HOW TO DRAW PEOPLE, CATS ROBOTS & BUILDINGS

Part One

HOW TO DRAW PEOPLE

Alastair Smith

Edited by Judy Tatchell

Designed by Nigel Reece

Illustrated by Graham Potts, Derek Brazell, Kevin Lyles, Paddy Mounter, David Downton, Nicky Dupays, Louise Nixon and Chris West

Photographs by Jane Munro Photography

Contents

Consultant: Richard Johnson

Drawing people

Drawing people is tricky because bodies are made up of so many different shapes. Still, if you follow the steps in this book you will find that you can get good results.

As well as helping you draw lifelike pictures, the book covers techniques such as cartooning and fashion illustration. This page contains some general tips.

● Get people to pose as models for you to draw. This enables you to check sizes and shapes of bodies while you draw them. If you cannot find a model, try copying a photo.

● Always plan a drawing by making a rough sketch, with pencil. This way you can ensure that the whole picture fits on your paper. Get the shapes right before you draw details.

● Draw big, rather than small. By doing this, you will be less likely to draw cramped-looking pictures. Also, you will find it easier to get detail into your pictures.

● Keep a rough book and pencil with you. Whenever you get a chance, make sketches in it. Keep old rough books, so that you can look back and see how your skills progress.

Materials

It is best to colour your pictures with the materials that you find easiest to use. However, you might like to try using a range of materials. This picture shows some of the effects that can be made with the materials that were used for the pictures in this book.

Pencils

Pencils are available with a range of leads, from hard to soft. Medium leads (called HB) are ideal for rough sketching.

You will see a rough pencil sketch on page 8. More detailed pencil drawings are on pages 30-31.

Watercolours

Mixed with a little water, watercolour paints can look strong and vivid, like this part of the boy's sweater. The picture on page 24 shows another example of this effect, drawn in a different style.

When mixed with a lot of water, the colours can look watery and soft. The picture at the top of page 13 shows a painting in this style.

Crayons

Crayons can be used to create a range of effects. For instance, smooth, delicate shading helps to create a natural look, as shown on page 4. Hatching can give a loose, light feel to a picture. You will find more details about the technique of hatching on pages 10-11.

Gouache

Gouache paints are vivid and are useful for creating flat areas. Poster paints give a similar effect and are cheaper, but the range of colours is narrower.

Felt-tips

Felt-tips are suited to unreal styles, such as comic strip styles (see page 21).

3

Heads and faces

Your face is the most expressive part of your body. Below the skin there are lots of tiny muscles, which you use all the time to make different expressions. These pages will help you to draw realistic-looking faces.

A face from the front

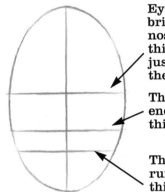

Eyes and bridge of nose go on this line, just above the centre.

The nose ends on this line.

The mouth runs along this line.

Start by sketching an oval shape, with a pencil. Then draw construction lines on it, as shown above.

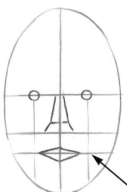

The tops of the ears are just above the eyes.

Draw a line down from the middle of each eye. The corners of the mouth will be near these lines.

Using pencil, plot rough shapes around the lines. Use these shapes as guides to help you sketch features.

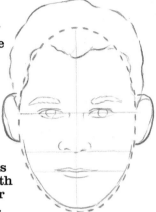

When you have drawn all the lines and shapes, start sketching features. Draw the hair as a single shape.

This picture is coloured with pencil crayons.

Colour the face and hair with a layer of pale colour. Start to build shade with more of the same colour.

Swirls of dark colour are added to the hair.

Instead of drawing hard lines around features, give them shape by adding shadow around them.

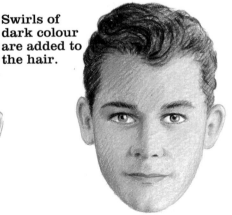

Use darker colours for areas in deep shadow. Add colour gradually until the face looks rounded.

4

Shading practice

It is quite difficult to make shading look convincing. For practice, draw and shade smooth, simple objects like those on the right. Look for light and shady parts before you begin.

Sketch the object in pencil first. Leave the white highlights blank, but colour the rest of the object with the lightest colour. Build up the shape by adding deeper shades of the same colour.

Heavier pressure was applied here to make the colour look darker.

Dark coloured crayons were used to colour the most shadowy parts.

Heads from different angles

The shapes here show you how to vary the construction lines in order to draw heads from different angles.

For raised and lowered heads, use curved lines to help you draw features in their correct positions.

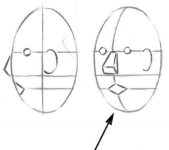

A drawing from this angle is known as a three-quarter view.

A drawing from the side is called a profile.

Artist's tip

For practice, try drawing and shading features on their own, in close-up.

There is a selection of features for you to copy on pages 30-31.

Drawing bodies

What someone looks like depends just as much on their body proportions*, the way they stand and their clothes, as on their facial features.

When you draw whole figures, the first stage is to do rough sketches. Plot the body shapes and positions before you draw them in detail and colour them in. Below, you can see the way in which the people on the right were drawn. You could choose one of these people and copy the stages.

Rough sketches

Rough sketches should be done in pencil, using shapes like those on the right. Before you start, try to imagine the body parts below the clothing. This will help you to see how the clothes hang when you draw them.

Start your sketch by drawing the main body shapes shown in red, then the limb shapes shown in blue.

Don't stop to erase your mistakes. Just carry on sketching lightly until you think that the overall body shape looks correct. Then draw the clothes outline, shown in green.

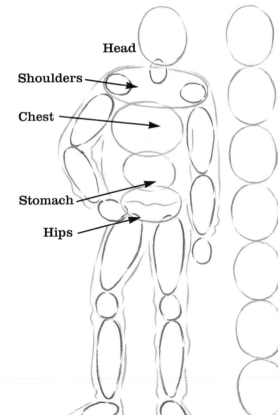

Head

Shoulders

Chest

Stomach

Hips

To check that the body parts in your sketch are in the right proportion, see how many head-sized ovals make up the overall height. If you are drawing an adult man, your subject will probably be about seven heads long.

Try doing rough sketches of some of the people at the top of this page. The more times you practise drawing body shapes like these, the easier they will become.

6 *When you are drawing a person, "proportion" means the size of one part of the body compared to another.*

Difficult angles

When a person is shown from a difficult angle, like the woman on the left, notice how some body shapes hide others. For instance, the head covers part of the shoulders, while the left arm hides the right arm.

Draw parts that are closer to you over the parts that they cover up. Rub out the parts that are covered.

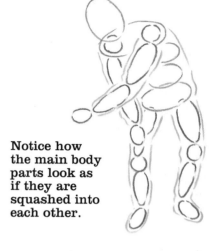

Notice how the main body parts look as if they are squashed into each other.

How many heads?

People's proportions depend, for instance, upon what age they are and whether they are male or female. This guide shows some average proportions.

Women are about six and a half head-lengths.

People in their mid-teens are about six head-lengths.

Four year olds are about three and a half head-lengths.

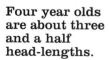

Shading clothes

The folds, shadows and highlights formed on clothes can make them difficult to draw.

Most folds occur at joints like the knees and elbows. Shadows are formed where folds dip inwards (such as on the elbows of this coat). Highlights form where folds catch the light. Highlights and shadows are usually curved, because they form around the body.

When you draw clothes, sketch the clothes shapes over body shapes. Then sketch folds and creases lightly in pencil before applying any colour.

Leave the highlighted areas white, but apply a thin layer of colour over the rest of the garment.

Extra layers of colour, plus streaks of darker colour, help to show shadows and folds on the clothes.

7

Using models

Often, artists get someone to pose as a model for them when they draw. This helps because it gives the artist time to concentrate on the shapes a body makes in a particular position. Ask people you know to model for you, so that you can sketch them. It is extremely useful drawing practice.

Model positions

Position your models so that they are comfortable, or they will not be able to hold a pose for long. Try to make sure that they do not have to pose for more than 15 minutes at a time.

Start by drawing a rough sketch. Concentrate only on making the shapes and proportions look correct. Make your sketch look about as finished as the one shown here. Do not stop to erase mistakes.

As you make your sketch, notice how the parts of the body fit together. Include the hidden body shapes in the sketch, to help you draw the model in the correct proportions.

More poses

You could try sketching these poses, or you could get someone you know to model in positions like them. Chat to your model while you sketch, to keep them from getting bored.

8

Transforming a model

Some artists use their sketches of models as bases for other pictures, complete with different clothes and a new background. You could use images from magazines, films and books to give you ideas for how to transform your models.

Skydiver

The skydiver's clothes were copied from pictures in a book. His boot treads were copied from hiking boots.

To provide the basis for the drawing, the model lay on the floor with his feet close to the illustrator, as shown here.*

Light, hazy shading makes this parachute look far away.

To make the body look as if it is coming towards you, the shading becomes stronger as it gets closer to the feet.

Bright colours help this picture to look exciting.

Shading practice

For extra shading practice, try drawing your models as if their bodies are a collection of smooth metal tubes and containers.

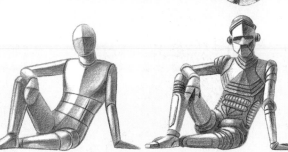

As a finishing touch you could add buttons, knobs, tubes and flashing lights, to turn your sketched figure into an android.

*The angle of this picture makes the body look distorted.
Find out more about drawing figures like this on pages 14-15.

Portraits

Portraits are detailed pictures of people. They are usually, but not always, fairly realistic and they may help to show the subject's personality.

Draw a portrait when your subject is relaxed and will sit still for a long time, for example, while he or she is reading, or watching television.

Starting the portrait

First, draw the rough head shape. Then sketch the body shapes in proportion to the size of the head. (See the panel on the right.)

To help you position the body parts correctly in relation to each other, check which parts line up with one another.

In this drawing the subject's right eye, right shoulder and right knee all line up. The right shoulder, left knee and left ankle also line up. In your portraits, sketch faint lines to help you keep the body parts lined up.

This portrait is shaded with crayons, using a technique called hatching. See the **Artist's tip** on the opposite page, for more about hatching.

Faint lines like these help to line up the body parts.

Checking proportions

To help work out the proportions, first look at the head, with one eye shut. Then measure it with a pencil held at arm's length, as shown.

Line up your thumb with the chin.

Use this measurement to see how many head-lengths make up the rest of the body.

Your portrait can be as big or small as you like. However, keep the number of head-lengths in the body the same in your portrait as in life.

10

Backgrounds

Use background colours that contrast with your subject, like the plain colours shown here. This will help people to focus on the subject of the portrait.

To help show your subject's personality, you could draw them with some of their favourite possessions.

Cameos

Cameos are silhouettes of heads drawn in profile, with crisp, accurate outlines. They look most effective if you make them small, like the one below.

First, sketch a head shape in pencil. Then plot the shape of the face and the hair.

Make the outline very clean and detailed. Keep checking against your subject.

For the finished effect, cut out an oval shape around the silhouette.

Artist's tip

Hatching is a technique well-suited to shading with pencils, crayons or pens.

Make lots of short, diagonal strokes. For faint shading, press down lightly. Space the hatches quite far apart.

Where shading is stronger, do hatches closer together. Press down quite hard to make the colours strong.

Where shading is strongest, try cross-hatching. Draw the hatches in a criss-cross pattern close together.

Special effects

Artists often arrange lights to help them create special effects with real models. These pages will show you how to create some special effects of your own. For best results, use angle-poise lamps or a bright flashlight.

Horror show

To make your model look like a terrifying character from a horror movie, shine a single light up from the floor, just in front of them.

Put the light on the floor, as shown in this photograph.

The light should be bright, to make shadows as sharp as possible.

Using watercolour

Apply watercolours in layers, called washes, starting with the lightest colour. Unless the previous wash is dry before you paint over it, the colours will blend. To create shadowy areas, add streaks of darker colour over a still-damp wash.

Grisly details

Add details, like a trickle of blood from the mouth and bloodshot eyes, to make the character complete.

For the background, use cold colours (see pages 18-19), like blues and greys, to give the scene a moonlit quality.

Artist's tip

Use gouache or poster paints when you paint details over watercolours (like the trickle of blood in this picture). These paints keep their true colours when used over watercolours.

True Romantic

For a romantic lighting effect, use two lights, as positioned in the photo below.

A light shone from behind the subject is called a backlight.

Position the backlight so that it gives a soft halo around the subject. The front light should be less bright. Use it to cut down the shadows on the face.

If you want to draw a particular mood, ask your model to imagine the mood and show it on their face. This subject looks sad, as if she is remembering a lost love.

Make your watercolours look soft, as in this picture, by mixing your paints with lots of water. If your mixture is too dark, the picture will look gloomy.

Mystery

To make a person look mysterious, like a prowling spy or private eye, shine a single light on them, from the side.

A light shone from the side is called a sidelight.

Clothes can help to set an atmosphere in a picture. Here, the subject is shown in a coat with a turned-up collar, to help him look suspicious.

Paint in black and white, with touches of light grey. To make shadows very dark, mix your black paint with hardly any water.

To look threatening, the model tilted his head and frowned.

Dramatic pictures

A picture can look dramatic if it captures movement, like the drawing on the right. Another way to make a picture look dramatic is to draw it from an unusual angle, like the one at the bottom of the opposite page.

Altering proportions

The picture on the right shows an example of how the proportions of body parts can look distorted when they are drawn from a certain angle. Because the front arm is stretched towards you, the right hand looks big in proportion to the rest of the body and the arm looks squashed. This effect is called foreshortening.

This picture shows off the skateboarder's balance and poise.

The skateboarder's left arm is also foreshortened.

To begin, sketch rough shapes. Start from the closest-looking part. Notice that closer parts cover up parts that are further away.

Rub out parts which have other parts in front of them. This helps you to see how to draw and shade your final version.

Foreshortening

As an example of foreshortening, notice how, as this person's arm raises, it seems to get shorter.

The distance between the raised hand and the body looks squashed. The hand looks large, as it is closer to you than before.

Drawing foreshortened figures is tricky. Practise the technique by sketching rough shapes only.

Action pictures

A picture of an exciting event looks really effective if you show it at the most action-packed moment, or even a split-second before, to add a feeling of suspense. Below are some action pictures drawn from dramatic angles.

Practice tip

Practise foreshortening by sketching long objects from various angles.

For further practice you could try drawing parts of yourself, like an arm, leg or hand.

Adding details

When you draw a dramatic picture, try to include details which will add atmosphere and excitement to the event. The labels show how drama can be added to a picture.

Body positions. Here, the leg positions suggest that the man is swinging from the ledge.

Facial expressions. Here, the face shows the person's grim determination to hang on to the wall.

Background. Here it shows a terrifying situation from a very dramatic angle.

15

People in perspective

Perspective drawings are based on the fact that the further away things are, the smaller they look. Things in the background are made to look as if they are the right size and in the correct position, compared with things in the foreground. On the opposite page, notice how the railway track, trees and people all look smaller as they get further away. The railway track disappears at a point (called the vanishing point) in the middle of the picture. Nothing is visible beyond the vanishing point.

Sketching a scene

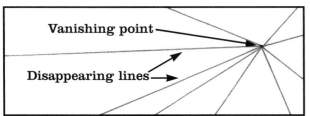

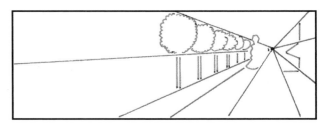

Start by drawing the vanishing point. Next, sketch guide lines (called disappearing lines) from the vanishing point. They will help you to draw distant things in proportion to things that are close up.

Sketch the main features of the scene, using the disappearing lines as guides. In the picture on the right the buildings, railway track and trees have all been sketched in this way. See below for tips about drawing people in the scene.

People in a line

When showing people in a line, directly behind each other, sketch the closest person first.

Draw disappearing lines from the person's feet and head. Show the people behind inside these lines.

People not in a line

For people not directly behind one another, sketch an upright line inside the disappearing lines, level with

where you want another person to go. Draw horizontal lines across from this, where the lines meet.

Creating depth

This scene was drawn in a comic style. (There are more details about comic styles on pages 20-21.) The unfinished parts of this scene should help to show how it was constructed. The tips dotted around the picture show several ways in which you can give an impression of distance in a scene.

In a realistic picture, colours get paler towards the horizon. Comic colouring is usually simpler, though, so the same colours are used in the foreground and background in this picture.

Repeated objects reinforce the sense of perspective.

Draw repeated objects closer together as they go into the distance.

People and objects in the foreground are drawn in more detail than in the background.

Put some figures partly in front of others. This connects the figures and leads your eye into the picture.

Using colour

The colours you use will affect the mood of a picture. You can make the mood more obvious by drawing and colouring in a particular style.

Baggy suit

The trumpet player is wearing a 1940s baggy suit. The colours suggest the atmosphere of a dimly lit jazz club. The drawing style emphasizes the size and bagginess of the suit.

Felt-tips were used to create strong, simple blocks of colour. These blocks give the picture a bold feel.

Notice how all the shapes look angular, especially at the shoulders, elbows and knees.

Drawing the figure

Sketch the rough body shapes first, in pencil.

Draw the clothes and their folds with mostly straight lines, around the body shapes.

Use the fold lines as guides to divide your drawing into areas of different shades.

Cold and warm colours

Colours are sometimes described as cold or warm. This is because people associate certain colours, such as blues and greys, with cold things, such as steel or the sea. They associate oranges, yellows and reds with warm things, such as fire and the Sun.

Cold colours

18

High speed skier

The skier's clothes are coloured with streaks of crayon, to make it look as if she is travelling very fast. Most of the clothes' colours are bright and warm. When used on this subject, they help convey a feeling of danger and excitement.

Building the colour

Begin by shading the lines quite far apart, as shown here. Leave highlight areas with hardly any lines.

Build up colour in darker areas by drawing the lines closer together.

Add darker shades over light shades to create shadows. The light and dark areas will make the body look solid.

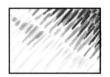

The warm coloured clothes stand out against the cool coloured background. If you want a background colour to contrast with the subject, colour the subject first and then choose a suitable, contrasting colour for the background.

Warm colours

In pictures, colours help to create atmospheres linked with coldness or warmth. For example, the blues in the picture on the previous page make it look sharp and cool. The woman's coat shown on page 6 is coloured in a warm colour to make it look cosy.

Comic strip people

Comic strips first appeared about a hundred years ago, in newspapers. Since then, several different styles of comic drawing have become popular. On these pages are examples of two of the most popular styles.

◄ Tintin, a daring young crimefighter, with his dog Snowy. Tintin's clothes are drawn in detail but his head is not. His simple facial features make him look honest and friendly.

"Funnies" style

The style of characters like those on the right was first used in newspapers in the USA, where comic strips in newspapers are called "funnies". The characters usually look silly to match the crazy adventures that they have.

The figures on the right show typical "funnies" features. You could use these examples to inspire you when you draw characters of your own.

Asterix the Gaul's headgear ► and dagger show that he is a warrior. However, his huge, rounded features and cheerful face make him look funny not threatening.

◄ Minnie the Minx, a mischievous character from the British comic *The Beano*. Her mouth, knobbly knees and wild expressions emphasize her cheeky sense of humour.

Comic drawing stages

Whatever comic drawing style you use, follow these steps when you create a character. Take time to work out the shape and expression of your character, so that it looks as interesting as possible.

To develop ideas for a character's look and personality, do a series of doodles.

Next, choose the position for your character, then make a sketch of it in pencil.

Superhero style

The first superhero-style comic character was Flash Gordon. He was first drawn in the 1930s. The superheroes shown here were created for Marvel comics in the 1960s.

Superheroes

Superheroes are very fit and muscular and they have abilities that ordinary humans cannot match. Their heights are about nine head-lengths, which exaggerates the power of their bodies. Their faces are usually handsome.

Some superheroes hide their true identities beneath masks. Most wear a tight-fitting costume when they perform their heroics.

You could try your own versions of the poses shown here. Design your own costumes for the superheroes to wear.

Spider-Man. His special powers enable him to climb up anything and spin enormous webs. Often, he uses his webs to trap criminals.

Sue Richards, member of a crime-fighting group called the Fantastic Four. She has the power to disappear, so she is also known as the Invisible Girl. Notice how her colour fades as she becomes invisible.

 Complete the sketch by adding details like facial features, expressions and clothes.

 Go over your pencil lines with a fine ink pen. Then rub out any pencil lines.

 Colour the clothes with strong, bright colours. Felt-tips are ideal.

Caricatures

Caricatures deliberately overstate a person's features to make them look funny. The best ones also manage to highlight the subject's personality. These pages will show you how to make your own caricatures.

Before you start drawing, imagine the person that you want to caricature. Remember which features make the strongest impression in your mind. Make those features the most obvious ones in your caricature.

Building a caricature

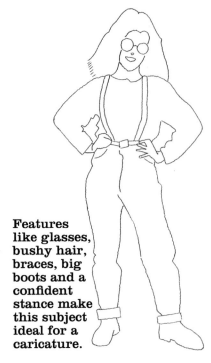

Features like glasses, bushy hair, braces, big boots and a confident stance make this subject ideal for a caricature.

Start by tracing or copying an original photo or life-like illustration. Show the important features of the original picture. Simplify the picture by using as few lines as possible. Do not show any shading.

When you have done your simplified drawing, decide how you want to alter your subject. Then trace your simplified drawing, making changes to the sizes and shapes of features to change the person's look.

Enlarge some features and shrink others. To enlarge a feature, trace slightly outside the lines of the previous drawing (for example, see the head and glasses above). To shrink a feature, trace inside it.

Celebrities

Famous people (like these movie stars) make good subjects for caricatures. Their larger-than-life personalities should give you a clue to how to exaggerate their features.

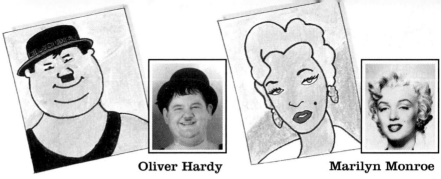

Oliver Hardy

Marilyn Monroe

Notice how the shapes have simplified and changed. For instance, hair is more bushy, glasses have grown, legs are longer and the boots are huge now.

Keep doing new tracings, altering the features at every stage, until you think that your caricature is extreme enough. After several stages of tracing, the drawing should have altered drastically.

Make sure that the original subject can be recognized in the final drawing. Ink and colour the caricature in the same way as a comic character. (See pages 20-21 for how to do this.)

New adventures

You could show caricatures in crazy, comic-style situations and adventures.

Sketch the rough body positions, then draw the caricature's features and clothes over the shapes.

Fashion illustration

Fashion illustrators draw people in styles which make clothes look as glamorous as possible. They usually base their illustrations on elegant figures that are at least eight heads long.

Sketching the pose

First, sketch a posing model. You could base your sketch on a photo from a fashion magazine. Show the proportions of a real person.

To make the drawing look more thin and elegant, sketch versions with lengthened body parts, especially the arms and legs.

Draw the outlines of clothes over the body sketch. Simplify the clothes shapes, to give your picture a sleek appearance.

Colouring the sketch

To paint a picture in watercolours, like the one on the left, follow these steps:

1. First, colour the skin tones and hair colour. Mix your paint with a lot of water, to make the colours look watery. Colour shapes like the knees with slightly darker tones, using a minimum of detail.

2. To colour the clothes, mix the paint with only a little water. Paint with bold brushstrokes and do not try to show close detail. Exaggerate highlights by leaving large areas of white (as on the left leg). Paint simplified shadows on top of the clothes colour.

3. When the clothes and skin colours have dried, give dark outlines to the picture. Try to paint these lines with single brushstrokes. This will make the body shape look fluid and curved. Also, add dark lines to the hair to give it texture.

4. Draw the details (like facial features and ear-rings) last, when the paint is dry. Sketch them in pencil and then draw over them with a fine ink pen.

Collage

In a collage, portions of coloured paper are cut out and stuck down instead of using paints. For a stylized effect, the shapes should be cut with jagged edges.

Building the collage

Sketch the pose and then lengthen the body shapes, as you would do for a fashion illustration. Add clothes shapes to the sketch.

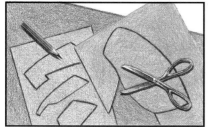

Trace the final sketch on to coloured paper. Cut out the tracings, making your cuts as straight as possible.

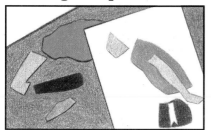

Glue the cut-out pieces of paper on a fresh piece of paper or card. Then follow the tips on the right to create a finished collage.

As an alternative, you could use a felt-tip pen to emphasize the shapes.

Stick smaller bits of coloured paper on to the larger pieces for details, like the stripes on this soccer kit.

Sketch the body and facial features over the stuck down paper, using simple, flowing lines to create the shapes.

Paint over the sketched lines with black watercolour, mixed with a little water. Use a thin brush and paint with light, fast sweeps of the brush.*

You can paint a variety of thick and thin lines, depending on how hard you press on the brush.

A colour patch behind the figure suggests the background.

Painted features do not have to follow the paper shapes.

Egyptian-style art

It can be amusing to use an art style that is inappropriate to your subject matter. For instance, the picture opposite shows a visit to a modern dentist, done in the style of an Ancient Egyptian painting.

This page points out some features of the Ancient Egyptian style, which was used about 3,000 years ago.

Style guide

Ancient Egyptian art does not show any perspective. People in the background are painted higher up the page but the same size as people in the foreground.

Figures never show any foreshortening. Things are shown either from the front or the side. When people are shown, their shoulders face outwards while their faces, stomachs and legs are shown from the sides.

Ancient Egyptians usually drew their pictures on stone walls, or on pieces of paper (called papyrus) made from strips of reed. To show a similar texture to these, draw your scene on rough brown paper or ordinary brown wrapping paper.

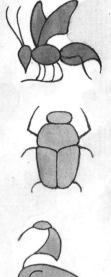

Important people are painted larger than ordinary people.

Often, large animals are shown smaller than humans, to symbolize that humans were thought to be more important than animals.

Usually, people are made to look skinny and long in proportion to their heads.

Notice how the hair and face are simplified. Faces do not show any feelings.

Hieroglyphics

The simplified objects above are examples of hieroglyphics, a written code made up of symbols and pictures. Ancient Egyptian artists used them to help explain their pictures to the viewer.

A trip to the dentist

Use watercolours to colour a picture in this style. For the clothes, paint in flat washes, using earthy, natural looking shades in keeping with the colours in an Ancient Egyptian picture.

You could paint a textured background on white paper, using very watery washes. To create a smudged effect, paint each new wash while the previous one is still damp.

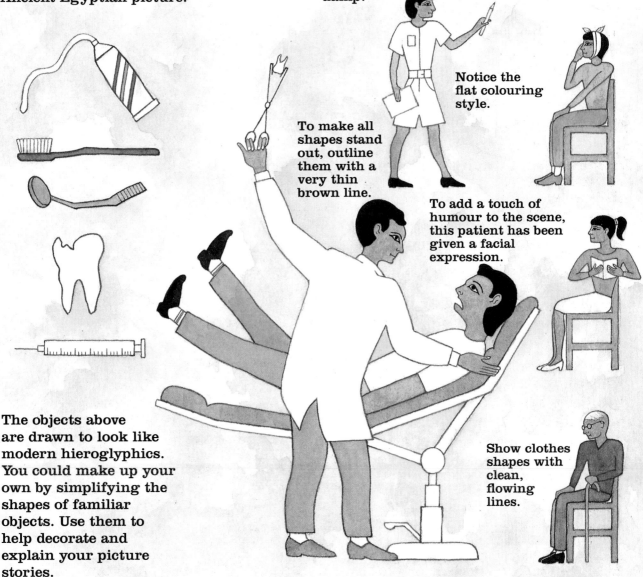

Notice the flat colouring style.

To make all shapes stand out, outline them with a very thin brown line.

To add a touch of humour to the scene, this patient has been given a facial expression.

The objects above are drawn to look like modern hieroglyphics. You could make up your own by simplifying the shapes of familiar objects. Use them to help decorate and explain your picture stories.

Show clothes shapes with clean, flowing lines.

Making masks

If you like drawing people, you will probably enjoy making masks. A mask hardly ever looks like a real face, but it highlights and exaggerates certain elements of a face to ensure that it has lots of character.

Masks are not difficult to make. All you need is some thin, flexible card, some elastic, scissors and a pencil and crayons, felt-tips or pens.

Mask-making steps

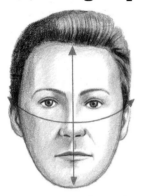

Start by measuring the face of the person who will wear the mask.

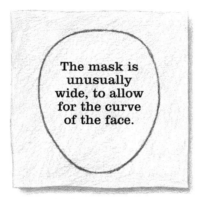

The mask is unusually wide, to allow for the curve of the face.

Draw the face shape on your card, according to your measurements.

Draw hair over and around the original design shape.

Do not draw face shadows on your mask. Real shadows will form on it when it is worn.

Plot the features in pencil. Colour the mask, then cut it out.

Holding the mask on

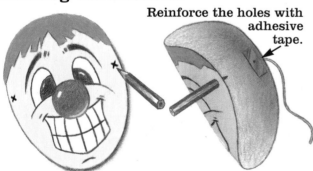

Reinforce the holes with adhesive tape.

Mark the positions for two holes, about 1cm (almost ½in) in from the widest points on either side of the mask.

Use the point of a pencil to make holes in the mask. Push elastic into the holes and tie it in place with knots.

Making eye holes

Work out where eye holes should go. Carefully, mark the positions for the eye holes with a pencil.

Pierce tiny eye holes in the mask. The holes do not have to be in the same place as the eyes of the mask design.

28

Mask styles

Masks can be just for fun but in some parts of the world people wear them for superstitious reasons or during religious ceremonies or festivals, such as carnivals.

The actors in some traditional forms of drama wear masks which show the identities of the characters. Here are some ideas that you could copy or adapt.

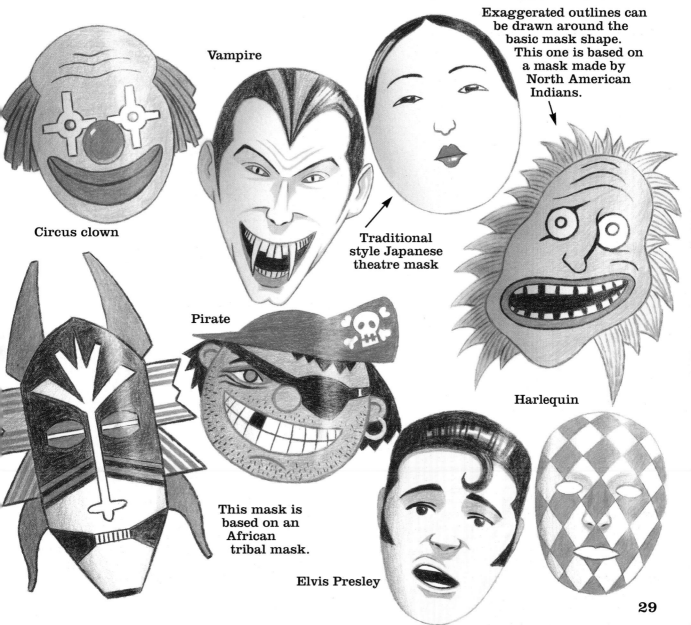

Circus clown

Vampire

Exaggerated outlines can be drawn around the basic mask shape. This one is based on a mask made by North American Indians.

Traditional style Japanese theatre mask

Pirate

Harlequin

This mask is based on an African tribal mask.

Elvis Presley

29

Body parts to copy

Many people spoil a well-proportioned picture by making mistakes when they draw the features in detail. To avoid this problem, practise drawing close-ups of features as often as you can, copying them from life or from photos.

You could copy the body parts on these pages for practice. Do not colour them in – concentrate on drawing the shapes, highlights and shadows. You could even use these shapes in your own pictures.

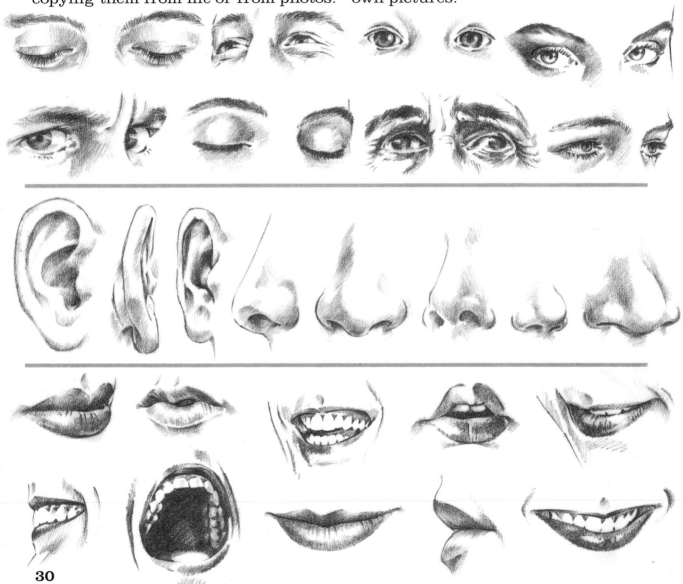

31

Moving figures to copy

Instead of copying these drawings line by line, try sketching the basic body shapes first, as shown on page 6. This is likely to result in a more lifelike picture than a direct copy. As you draw the basic shapes, keep looking at the finished version on this page to help you.

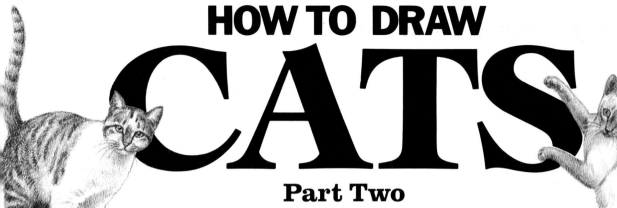

HOW TO DRAW
CATS

Part Two

Lucy Smith

Designed by Fiona Brown

Illustrated by Chris Chapman

Additional designs by Iain Ashman

Additional illustrations by Derick Bown

Cartoon illustrations by Jo Wright

Contents

About drawing cats

Cats make wonderful pictures with their sleek bodies and graceful, nimble movements. The next part of the book shows you how to draw all sorts, from tiny kittens to fierce tigers.

Wild cats are on pages 52-55 and 63.

Because cats spend a lot of time on the move, they are a challenge to draw well. Copying photos or pictures of cats will help you practise.

The copying method at the bottom of the page is a good way to start. It works for any picture.

For kittens, see pages 50-51.

Pages 42-47 show some typical cat moods and action poses.

Copy cats

Tape the top edge of the overlay down with masking tape, which lifts off without tearing.

Look for the shapes shown in red first, then the green, then the blue.

Flip up the overlay to check any details that are unclear.

Cats may look hard to draw, but you can break them down into simple shapes. Try this copying technique. It is better than tracing a picture because it helps you understand how a cat's body is made up.

Lay a sheet of tracing paper over the picture and fasten it as shown. Looking through it, try to pick out basic shapes that make up the cat's body. Draw them on the tracing paper overlay with a soft pencil.*

*Any pencil coded HB, 1B, 2B, 3B, 4B or 5B will do.

Sketching cats from life

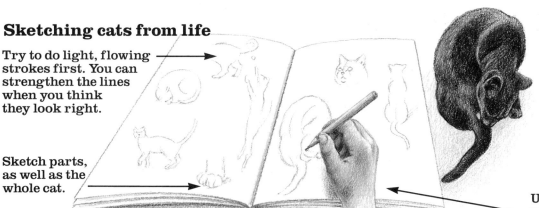

Try to do light, flowing strokes first. You can strengthen the lines when you think they look right.

Sketch parts, as well as the whole cat.

Look closely at how the body is stretched or curved, at the angle of the head and the position of the legs and tail.

Use soft pencils for quick lines.

Sketching live cats is a good way to practise watching and drawing them. As you sketch, don't stop to rub things out; work on getting the main lines right and keeping your strokes flowing. You can put more detail in later.

You could sketch wild or big cats (see pages 52-55) at a zoo or safari park. If you have a video recorder, try taping a TV programme about them. Replay it and use the "pause" button to freeze the action while you sketch the animals.

Once you have worked out the basic shapes, you can make them bigger or smaller to change the size of the cat.

When you have done the outline, rub out the basic shapes.

Take the overlay off the original picture. Tidy up the outline, referring to the original for help. You can either add details and colour on the overlay, or retrace the outline on thicker paper first.

Try copying this tiger using the method on the left and the shapes shown above right.

What to look for

This picture shows the main points to look for when drawing a cat. As you draw, it helps to think of the cat as made up mostly of simple, rounded shapes. Try to use smooth, curving lines to bring out its graceful build.

The head is quite small compared with the body. It is held high and forward, which helps the cat to see and smell its prey when it hunts. The skull is fairly broad and rounded on top.

The spine is long and so supple that the cat can arch its back nearly double without hurting itself.

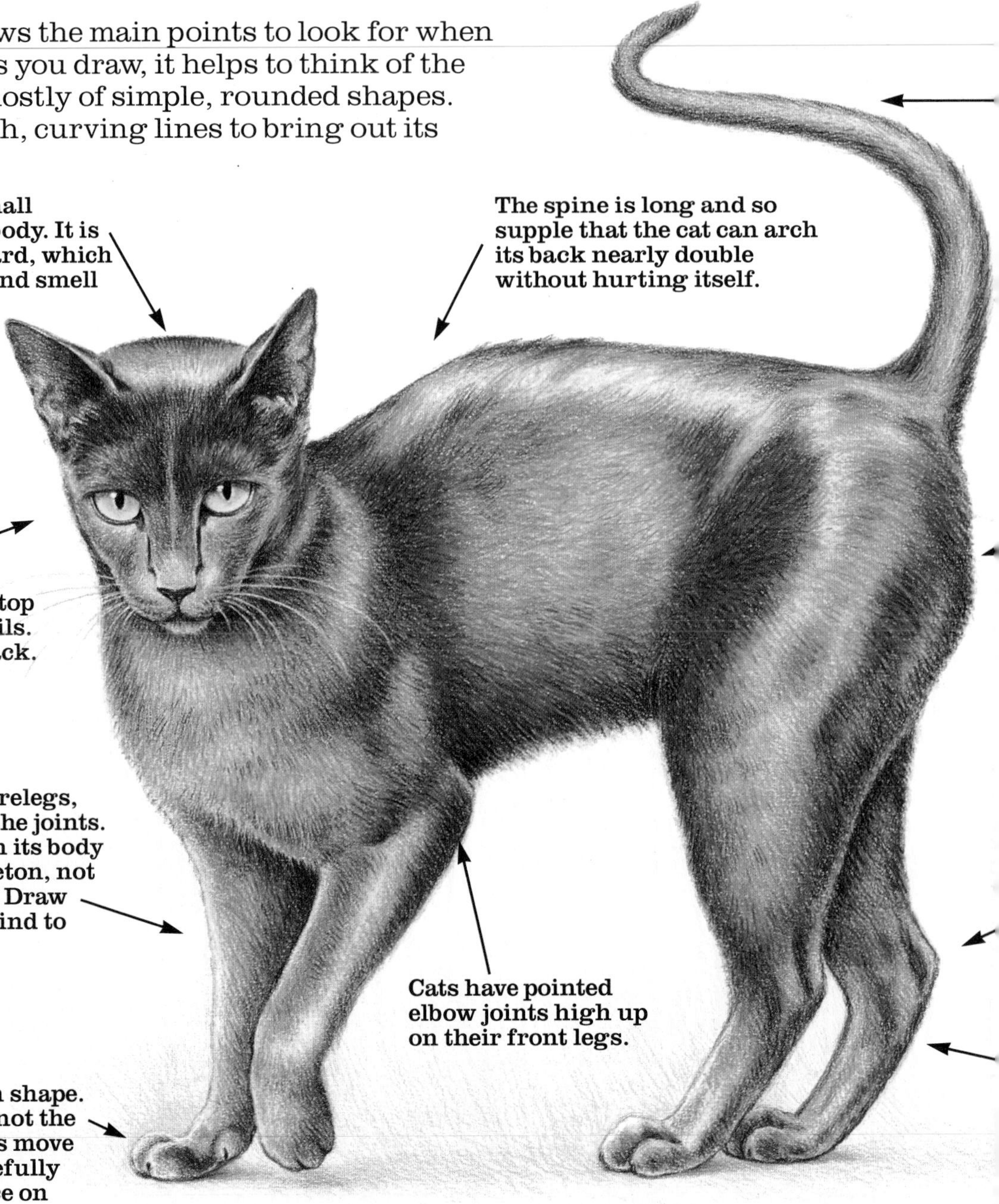

Colour the eyes yellow-green. Add darker green at the top and around the pupils. Make these solid black.

The front legs, or forelegs, are very flexible at the joints. All the cat's legs join its body high up on the skeleton, not just at tummy level. Draw them with this in mind to make the lines flow.

Cats have pointed elbow joints high up on their front legs.

The paws are oval in shape. They are only toes, not the cat's whole feet. Cats move so lightly and gracefully because they balance on their toes.

Most cats have tails almost as long and supple as their spines. The tail is really an extension of the spine, so try to make the two flow in a continuous line.

The hips or hindquarters are very muscular, which is why cats can spring so far and fast. You can find out how to make them look muscular below.

These pointed joints are the cat's heels, called hocks. They stick out backwards when it is standing up, but rest on the ground when it sits.

The muscles under the skin make the curves you see on the surface. You can make a short-haired cat like this look muscular by shading faint lines in a darker colour.

Drawing the cat

Using a soft pencil, draw the big ovals of the body, chest and hindquarters first, and the smaller head circle. Add the legs, paws and tail, then the face and ears.*

The line of the cat's belly is almost straight.

The legs join the body high up.

Refine the shapes to get the cat's outline. Apply pale grey-blue as a base. Let the paper show through on the lightest parts to give a sheen to the fur.

Use colour pencil or watercolour wash for the base.

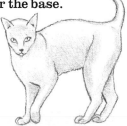

Add detail to the face*: colouring the eyes helps bring it to life. Darker grey shadows give the cat form (see the tips on the right).

Professional tips

Proportions. To help you get the proportions and outline right, look at the space in between parts of the cat: for example, the shape of the space framed by the cat's tummy and legs, and the space between its hindlegs.

Shadows. Adding shadows to your drawing helps to make the cat look three-dimensional and rounded. You need to shade the parts which the light does not fall on directly.

It helps to imagine the cat's body as a cylinder.

Direction of light.

Direction of light.

Mark arrows on your drawing to show the direction of the light. This helps you work out which parts of the cat should be in shadow.

*You can find out how to draw a cat's face in detail on pages 38-39

Drawing the head and face

Cats use all their facial features in many ways to show their moods, so drawing the face well adds character and life to your pictures. Here you can see how to structure the head. Opposite are more hints about how to draw the cat's main features in detail to get a really convincing look.

A cat's head

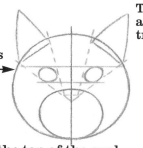

Horizontal lines make sure the eyes are level. →

The ears are triangles.

The broken outline gives a furry effect.

Use a soft pencil.

Draw a circle. Do a vertical line down the middle to help you position the features evenly on each side of the face. Add a small oval in the lower part of the circle for the muzzle.

Near the top of the oval, draw a little upside-down triangle for the nose. Draw wedge shapes out from this to the rim of the head circle to help you place the eyes and ears as shown.

Add the mouth as an upside-down Y-shape. Rub out the construction lines. Colour the head pale fawn, fanning your pencil or brush strokes out from the middle to follow the lie of the fur.

Shade under and around the muzzle to help bring it out from the face. Refine the outlines and add detail to all the features (see below and opposite).

To colour the eyes, do a layer of yellow, then orange. Add brown shadows. If you use paint, let each layer dry before applying the next. Do black pupils.

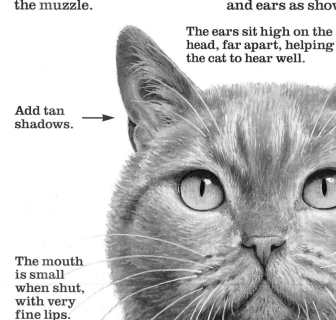

The ears sit high on the head, far apart, helping the cat to hear well.

Add tan shadows. →

The mouth is small when shut, with very fine lips.

The eyes are big and widely spaced.

The nose and eyes together form a V-shape.

Draw the whiskers last, in white.

38

Eyes

The most striking things about a cat's face are its eyes. They give an immediate impression of its character. Here is some help with making them look alive.

The eyes are spheres so the highlight falls in the same place on each one.

You can make the eyes look more intense and realistic by colouring them darker at the top and lighter towards the bottom. Adding a white highlight to each eye makes it look bright and luminous.

In dim light, the pupil* widens and is circular, filling most of the eye.

In good light, it is a medium-sized vertical oval.

In strong light, it becomes a narrow slit.

Cats' pupils change size and shape depending on how much light there is. This helps the cat to see better.

Nose

The nose is small with a triangular, hairless tip called the "nose leather". This is very sensitive to touch, so cats use it to examine things.

Do the nostrils darker to make them look hollow.

Do tiny dots of colour very close together to build up a textured effect on the nose leather. This technique is called stippling.**

Whiskers

The whiskers are extremely sensitive. The cat uses them to touch things and to sense changes in the air around it.

Do a few single whiskers above the eyes.

Do little dots where each whisker grows.

Most of the whiskers grow in several rows on each side of the muzzle. They twitch, bristle or flatten depending on how the cat feels. They are usually white.

Ears

Cats' ears can pick up the tiniest squeak of a mouse or chirp of a bird. They are quite big and cone-shaped so they catch sounds easily.

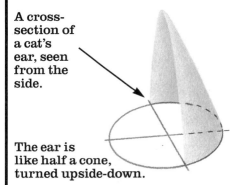

A cross-section of a cat's ear, seen from the side.

The ear is like half a cone, turned upside-down.

Each ear can twitch separately sideways, back or forwards to focus on where a sound is coming from.

Do longer, lighter hairs here.

Shading along the outer edge makes the ear look three-dimensional.

Cats often have longer hairs along the inner edge of each ear. Inside, the ear has little or no fur, so the skin is paler. Do the innermost bit darker though to give it shape.

*The pupil is the dark bit in the middle of the eye.
**See page 41.

Fur and markings

The only parts of a cat's body not covered with fur are the tip of its nose and its paw-pads, so it is worth practising drawing fur in detail to get a life-like effect. Here you can see ways to do the main types.

Drawing different types of fur

For short fur, pick out the palest colour in the coat and apply it in either light pencil or a watercolour wash (see opposite). When it is dry, add lots of short, close strokes of darker colour.*

Colour long fur in the same way as short, but use longer, looser strokes. Group several strokes together as shown to get a tufted effect. Make them flow down rather than along the sides of the body.

Rex cats (see page 49) have curly fur. To draw it, do short, arched strokes very close together in rows over the base colour. Let this show through in between the rows for a rippling, shiny look.

Common colours and markings

Tabby cats have pale coats with dark stripes. Start by applying the base colour. When it is dry, add the stripes. Make them follow the curves of the cat's body (see pages 42 and 51).

To draw a white cat on pale paper, use coloured shading to give it shape. Try warm fawns or yellows to get a sunlit or firelit effect, or cool blues if the cat is in moonlight or shadow.

For cats with white patches, colour the darker areas of the coat first, letting some white show around the edges where the dark and light hairs overlap. Then add soft shading on the white parts.

Make your strokes follow the direction of the fur, pointing along the body.

Techniques and materials

Below are examples of different drawing methods and materials which create convincing furry effects. Use a sharp pencil or fine brush to draw single hairs.

Coloured pencils

Hatching is lots of short, straight lines done side by side close together. It is good for short, sleek fur.

Cross-hatching is layers of short lines going in different directions. It gives a dark, dense look, useful for shadows.

Blocking means using the side of the pencil point to get a flat area of colour with no gaps showing.

Coloured pencils used on a rough-textured paper give a broken, fuzzy line which is good for fluffy or long fur.

On hard paper, scratch through coloured pencil or wax crayon with a sharp compass point to do fine white hairs.

Watercolours

The damp paper helps the colour blend in and gives a more even tone.

A watercolour wash is a quick way to do the first layer of colour. First mix the paint. With a soft, thickish brush, wet the paper with water. When it has soaked in but is still damp, put plenty of colour on the brush. Starting at the top of the page, do bold, quick strokes to and fro ◀ until you reach the bottom.

Stippling. With a small, blunt brush, do masses of tiny dots of colour close together. A stiff brush works well, or cut the tip ◀ off a soft one.

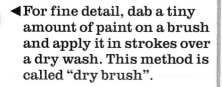

Stiff brush

Soft brush

◀ For fine detail, dab a tiny amount of paint on a brush and apply it in strokes over a dry wash. This method is called "dry brush".

◀ Wet watercolour. Apply paint to a wet paper or wash to get a blurred, soft effect which is good for drawing realistic-looking markings.

Moods and expressions

Cats are very expressive and use their whole bodies to show how they feel. These two pages show some typical moods to draw, and give you tips on how to make them look really vivid.

Do the red shapes first, then the green, then the blue.

Do triangles for the ears.

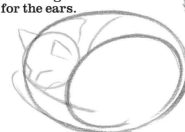

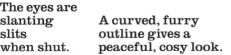

The eyes are slanting slits when shut.

A curved, furry outline gives a peaceful, cosy look.

Sleepy

A cat curled up snugly like this in a ball is a fairly easy subject to draw, because the whole picture makes an oval shape.

In pencil, do the basic shapes as shown. Refine the outlines, then build up the tabby markings using the method on page 40. Use

pastels or watercolours to get a soft, gentle feel. A pinky haze around the cat and orange highlights on its fur suggest a fireside glow.

Aggressive

The tail is up and the back is arched.

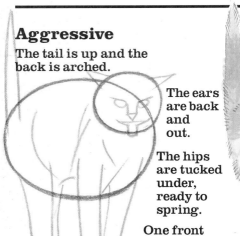

The ears are back and out.

The hips are tucked under, ready to spring.

One front paw is poised to lash out.

Short, sharp strokes here make the fur look bristly.

The cat stands sideways with its fur out to look bigger.

Whiskers held up, forwards and out exaggerate the snarl.

Add the teeth in white poster paint when the other colours are dry.

Claws out.

A threatened cat may react aggressively like this. As you do the basic shapes, note how this pose makes the cat look as big as possible.

Go over the outlines, making them bold and strong to suggest the fierce mood and add impact to the picture. Apply pale fawn as a base.

This mottled coat pattern is called tortoiseshell. Build it up by adding patches of gold, rust, dark brown and black once the base is dry.

Alert

Because you are seeing this cat almost head on, you need to draw the parts nearest to you bigger than the rest. To make the front and back legs look as if they are lined up behind each other, close the gaps between them. This is called foreshortening.*
To get this pose right, trace the basic body shapes carefully.

The cat is upright with its head and tail held high.

The head looks big as it is nearest.

The body ovals overlap to bring the front and back legs close together.

Bold shapes make the drawing look lively.

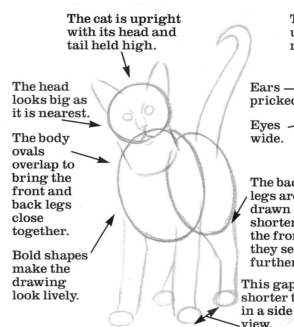

The tail is curved up like a question mark.

Ears pricked.

Eyes wide.

The back legs are drawn shorter than the front so they seem further away.

This gap is shorter than in a side view.

Frightened

Try to work out the basic shapes of this frightened cat for yourself. Its whole body is tense and crouching back as it cowers away in terror.

Arched back.

Ears flat.

Head down.

For spiky fur, draw short, straight lines out from the middle of the body.

Curved tail.

Chin in.

Legs bent.

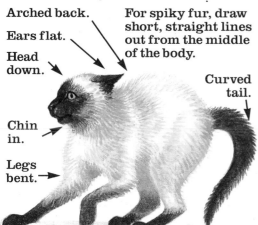

Relaxed

Try drawing this contented cat in white on black or dark paper. First work out the basic shapes and draw them in white pencil. Apply a thin wash of white watercolour paint all over. When it is dry, leave this layer to show through on the shadowy parts and build up the palest areas, or highlights, with white crayon.

Let the paper show through to mark the line of the chin.

Do long, loose lines for a supple look.

Add a patterned rug in coloured pencils to make an eye-catching background.

*There is more about foreshortening on page 47.

Cats in action

Cats are very agile, so drawing them in action is hard because they move fast and get into all sorts of acrobatic positions. Here is advice on getting a sense of movement into a drawing, as well as some action pictures to try.

Loping cat

Use soft pencil for speed.

Just do stick figures at this stage.

Place the head further forward.

Start with lots of quick, simple line sketches to try to get the basic position right. If the picture looks too static, as above, don't

Lengthen the neck.

Tilt the body slightly.

worry. Keep sketching until your lines start to flow. Exaggerating them a bit, as in this picture, can improve the sense of movement.

The tail is up. →

Draw some paws lifted to show the cat is in mid-stride.

The upright ears and tail add a sprightly touch.

The hind legs propel the cat forward.

▲ Once the basic lines are right, put in the body shapes as shown. Use a soft pencil and don't press hard at this stage: keep the lines light and flowing.

Improve the outlines, making them stronger and cleaner now to give a feeling of energy. Rub out any unwanted marks before applying a fawn base.

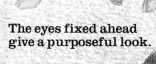

The eyes fixed ahead give a purposeful look.

Professional tip

Use the space around the cat to suggest movement, by keeping the background simple. A detailed one is distracting and slows the movement down by cluttering the picture and blurring the outlines.

The curving and stretching stripes increase the sense of moving muscles.

◀ Add shading as shown, then the russet stripes. Put in a couple of lines to show the ground level. This gives the raised paws an extra lift.

Sharpening claws

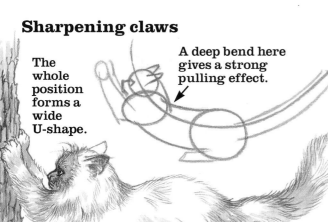

The whole position forms a wide U-shape.

A deep bend here gives a strong pulling effect.

For this picture, draw the cat first. Start by doing a curving line as shown to get the feel of the movement sweeping through the whole body from toes to tail. This line will also help you position the basic shapes.

Washing

Cats have such supple spines that they can bend almost double, like this, to wash their hindquarters. This position looks hard to draw because it is so contorted, but the basic shapes are quite simple.

The hind legs are stretched out in a V-shape.

The spine is curved almost into a circle.

Fighting

Try copying this picture, using the method on pages 34-35 to discover the basic body shapes. The tips here will help you position the cats.

The cat's back is parallel with the dark cat's left foreleg.

The shape of the whole picture is like a wide upside-down triangle.

For this cat, use bold curves to show how its whole body is coiled and arched ready to spring forward.

This cat is protecting itself. Its body is off-balance and its legs and tail stretched taut.

There are more action pictures to try on the next two pages.

45

The head is up, looking at where the cat aims to land.

Springing down

To draw this springing cat, do a long oval for the main part of the body, which is stretched as the cat reaches down to reduce the distance it has to drop. Notice that the chest and thigh ovals are parallel, showing how the cat has balanced itself perfectly for the leap. Its back legs are folded ready to push it off into ◄ the air.

Leaping

Cats can jump up to ► four or five times their own height. For this dynamic picture, draw the cat in the usual way. As you put in the shading,* add a shadow on the ground too. This is an easy but effective way of showing that the cat is high in the air.

A background of sky with no ground visible suggests the cat is high up and adds an element of risk to the picture.

The hind legs are long and taut. →

The tail is up and out to help the cat balance in the air.

Stretching

Cats nearly always stretch their whole bodies like this just after waking up. When you have drawn this cat, add a long, thin shadow under it as shown to increase the stretched look.

This smooth curve gives a supple feel.

The lifted forepaw gives a sense of movement.

Stalking

◀ Cats crouch down low like this to stalk their prey. You need to use foreshortening here because the cat is coming towards you. The parts you cannot see are still there, but hidden. Cats often hunt at night, and this moonlit background adds suspense to the picture. The moon is the light source, so put it in before you colour the cat to see where to shade and highlight the fur.

The eyes are fixed on its prey.

The whole position forms an S-shape.

Use bluish highlights, as the moon casts a cold, eerie light.

The cat would look like this from the side.

Draw in the slope when you do the basic shapes, as it affects the way the legs are positioned.

Rolling

Cats often roll over like this when they feel contented and safe. Here, the whole body is limp and relaxed, so make the lines fluid and soft to give a gentle feel. Although you are seeing the cat upside-down, draw it without turning the paper around. Do a fluffy rug as a background to add to the peaceful atmosphere.

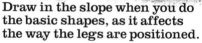

The top of the head is flatter where it touches the floor.

For the cat's fur, do tiny strokes in darker pencil when the base colour is dry.

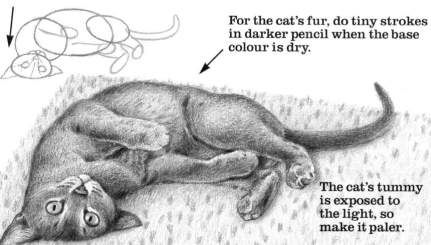

The cat's tummy is exposed to the light, so make it paler.

Different kinds of domestic cat

There are lots of different breeds of domestic or pet cat. They are all basically alike in build, but here you can see some important differences to watch out for when drawing specific types.

Domestic shorthairs

Many of the pet cats you see around are of this type, though they may not be pure-bred. Domestic shorthairs are solid and chunky with close, thick fur. They have rounded heads and bodies set on short, sturdy legs, and are bred in a huge range of colours. This one is a tortoiseshell. To colour it, follow the tips on page 42.

The eyes are very round and a deep copper colour.

The paws and tail-tip are blunt.

Oriental shorthairs

These cats also have short fur, but they are sleeker, slimmer and have longer limbs, muzzles and tails than domestic shorthairs. There are several distinct breeds, one of the most popular being the Siamese.

You can tell a Siamese by its pale body and darker face, legs and tail, which are called its points. One way to draw Siamese markings is with thick paper and watercolours. Dampen the paper slightly, then apply a very light grey or fawn wash. When this is nearly dry, add the darker points.

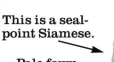

Use pinky-grey for the points of this lilac-point Siamese.

The eyes are a vivid deep blue.

The head is wedge-shaped, with a longish muzzle.

The paint will spread, or "bleed", a bit, so apply it over a smaller area than you actually need. For a soft, realistic look, dab it with a tissue to blend the edges into the wash.

This is a seal-point Siamese.

Pale fawn base.

Dark-brown points.

48

Rex cats

The body is slender and set on long, slim legs.

The tail is long, very thin and pointed.

The whiskers are very long and curved.

The paws are small and oval.

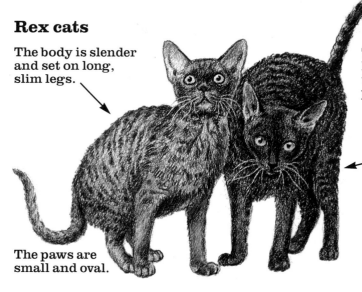

This unusual-looking breed has a silky, curly coat which grows in rippling waves. To draw this effect, it is best to use coloured pencils, which make it easier to control your lines. Use a paler colour for the base, then build up the darker shades on top in rows of short, curved lines to create a ridged look.

Longhaired cats

When drawing a longhaired cat like this smoke Persian, remember that under all its fur, its body is like any other cat's. So start with the basic shapes, but notice that in this breed, the head is a bit bigger in relation to the rest of the body.

Tiny ears

The legs are short and strong.

The body is solid and thickset.

The tail is very plumy.

Even in profile, these cats have such short noses that their heads fit easily into a circle.

For the smoke colour, apply a silver-grey base. Add streaks of darker grey along the back. Blend these with black on the face, legs and tail. Use the lines of the fur to give shape to the body.*

The fur grows in a long ruff around the neck and chest.

There is more about drawing long, short and curly fur on page 40.

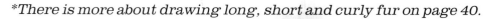

Kittens and cubs

Kittens make lovely, lively pictures. They are quite hard to draw, though, because their bodies are softer with less definite lines than adult cats'. They also have different proportions.

Four-week-old kitten

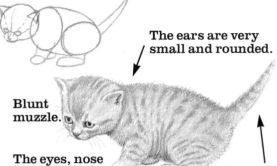

The ears are very small and rounded.

Blunt muzzle.

The eyes, nose and mouth are close together.

The tail is short and pointed.

Nine-week-old kitten

At this age, the ears are quite long and pointed.

The basic body shapes are very round.

Very young kittens like these have big heads in relation to their bodies.* Their legs are quite short and thick, with big paws. Kittens look cuddly as their fur is very soft. For a fluffy look, blur the outlines a bit so there are no hard edges.

A nursing cat and kittens

The cat and kittens form a fan-shape.

The kittens' heads and bodies overlap. The legs and paws are tucked away out of sight.

The wriggling tails add a lively touch.

The closed eyes give the cat a contented look.

For this grouping, position the mother cat before starting on the kittens. Use her front and back legs to help you put each kitten in the right place.

Use smooth, flowing lines to create a peaceful feeling. Notice how the cat's body is long and loose, while the kittens are rounded and tightly packed together.

Their different colours and markings also add interest. For each one, do the palest colours first, then the patches and stripes. For a soft look, use light strokes.

50   *Compare these kittens' proportions with the adult cat on page 36.*

Kittens at play

Kittens are bundles of energy and love playing. In the pictures below, look at how much movement and mood come from the paws, legs and tails.

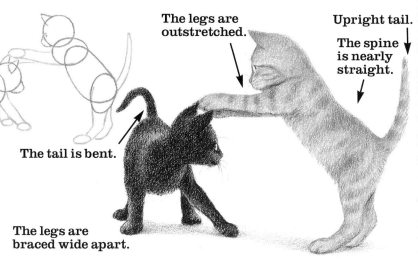

The legs are outstretched.

The tail is bent.

The legs are braced wide apart.

Upright tail.

The spine is nearly straight.

Draw the black kitten first. It is seen from the front, so you need to use foreshortening (page 43) to get it right. Its body is low and tense, ready to spring.

Its eye is fixed on the ball.

There is a smooth curve from the spine to the tail-tip.

To position the ginger kitten, look at the space between the two animals. The ginger one's body is parallel with the line of the other's left foreleg.

For this crouching position, draw the head and body shapes close together. Make the tabby stripes crinkly to give the body a compressed, coiled look.

The taut whiskers and flicked-up tail give the kitten a cheeky, playful air.

Cubs

Like domestic kittens, baby wild cats, often called cubs, look different from adults. Compare these two with the adult ones on page 53.

Lynx cub

The ears are very long with tufted tips.

The cheeks have not yet grown long fur.

The huge legs and paws make the cub look gawky.

Cheetah cub

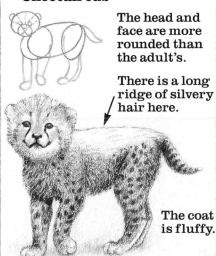

The head and face are more rounded than the adult's.

There is a long ridge of silvery hair here.

The coat is fluffy.

Wild cats

With their dramatic markings and powerful, elegant bodies, wild cats* make striking drawings. Though their size and colouring make them seem very different from pet cats, in fact they have a similar body structure.

Drawing heads

Use the construction method on page 38, but alter the shapes as shown to make these heads quite different.

European wild cat

For a savage look use wider, flatter shapes.

Use a broad triangle to place the ears.

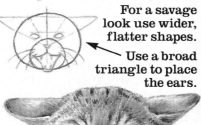

Narrowed yellow eyes.

Tiger

Do a longish oval for the muzzle.

The head is big and heavy.

Tiger

The back and neck form an almost straight line.

The tail is held low.

Slightly blurred stripes give a furry, rippling look.

The tiger is the biggest of all cats. It has a heavy head (see left) and body set on thick, strong legs. Try painting it with pale yellow-brown watercolour. Let this dry, then add red-brown as shown. While this is still damp, paint in the black stripes.

Serval

To draw this serval, it helps to think of it as like a pet cat with a very long neck, ears and legs. Use pale yellow for the base colour. Add light brown over it. Put the black spots on last.

Very small head.

Huge ears.

Powerful thighs.

The tail is quite long and thick.

Small paws.

White belly.

*Very large wild cats, such as lions (see pages 54-55), tigers and cheetahs, are known as big cats.

Cheetah

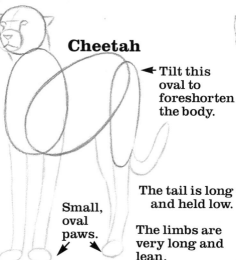

← Tilt this oval to foreshorten the body.

Small, oval paws.

The tail is long and held low.

The limbs are very long and lean.

In pencil, draw the basic shapes as above. The skull is flatter than other cats', so place the eyes higher up to suggest this.

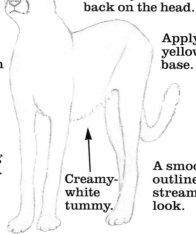

The tiny ears are set back on the head.

Apply a light yellow-fawn base.

Creamy-white tummy.

A smooth, clean outline gives a streamlined look.

Refine the outlines. Notice that the rib-cage is deep and the tummy tucks up under the hind legs, more like a dog's body.

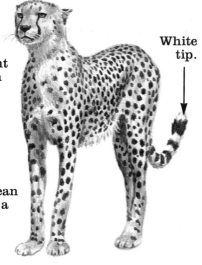

White tip.

Add shading as shown in light brown. Colour the eyes amber and the nose and lips black. Do the small, round black spots last.

Northern lynx

The eyes have white rims.

Squarish muzzle. →

Do faint spots here. →

The tail is very short.

This lynx has a shortish, heavy body and long legs with very powerful hindquarters. The long tufts of fur on its cheeks move according to its mood. Leave the underparts white and colour the head and upper body red-brown.

Drawing the details

Wild cats often have distinctive features like those below.

Put them in to add the finishing touch to your pictures.

The backs of tigers' ears are black with a bold white spot. ▶

A lynx has long black ◀ tufts at its ear-tips.

A cheetah has black lines running from its inner eye-corners to its lips. ▶

53

A pride of lions

Unlike most wild cats, lions live in groups, or prides, instead of alone. Here is a scene to copy. Opposite and below are suggestions for how to go about it, together with tips on drawing the lions' basic shapes.

A clear blue sky adds a feeling of heat. Do a pale blue base, then blend in darker blue pencil at the top.

Use a light sandy-fawn as the base for the landscape. Add warm oranges and browns over it.

The mountains in the distance frame the scene and give it a sense of scale. Do them in light violet, as colours look paler and bluer the further away they are.

Dark spots here.

The lions' tails add movement to the scene and guide the eye from one part to the next.

The three cubs form a roughly triangular shape.

This lioness and the seated one opposite face into the middle, which helps to frame the picture and focus your eyes on it.

Do the rich brown mane last, over a sandy base.

In real life this lion would be bigger than the lionesses, but you should draw him smaller here as he is further away.

The three lions in the middle are looking straight at you, giving the picture a strong focus.

54

How to copy the scene

In pencil, sketch in the line of the horizon. Then do the lioness nearest the front on the left. You can position and size up the rest in relation to her.* When you have drawn the whole scene, colour it in using the tips below. Work on the landscape and lions at the same time, so all the different colours are balanced and don't clash or merge together too much.

For the lions, use a pale sandy base with a mixture of gold and red-brown on top. Leave the chins white.

This young adult male's mane is not fully grown.

The way this lioness's head overlaps the young male helps to connect the two distant lions to the rest of the scene.

The basic shapes

Lions and lionesses have long muzzles, big, heavy heads and thick, powerful bodies.

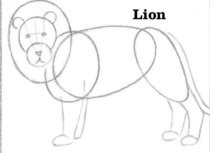

Lion

Use similar shapes as for a tiger (see page 52), but with bigger, rounder ears and an outer oval for the mane.

Lioness

Seen from the side, this lioness's body and legs form a triangle.

Squarish muzzle.

Cub

Lion cubs have rounded bodies and faces, with big heads and paws for their body size.

*There is more advice about arranging a picture on page 62.

55

Cartoon cats

Cats' strong characters, expressive faces and bodies and their habit of getting into comic scrapes as they roam make them ideal subjects for cartoons. Below and on the next three pages you can see how to draw cats in a cartoon style to make lively, funny pictures full of interest and action.

Cartoon cat

In pencil, start by doing the basic shapes as shown above. To get a comic look, exaggerate features like the eyes, teeth and claws and use strong, bold lines.

Zigzags make the outline look soft and fluffy.

Go over the outlines and features in waterproof black felt tip pen*, then lightly pencil in the inner edges of the markings. Try to keep all the lines clear and clean.

Leave the white markings blank and apply a base in light orange over the rest. When this dries, put in the stripes in darker orange. Use bright, solid colours to get a lively look: felt tips or coloured inks work best.

Add a bent whisker and a few stray hairs last, in black, to give the cat more character.

Colour the eyes bright green when you have done the markings. Add tiny black pupils when the green is dry.

A collar and name tag add a touch of extra colour and fun.

Give each marking a definite, crisp edge for a more striking effect. White patches on a bright coat make the cat look clownish.

*You could use ink to outline your finished drawing, but a felt tip is quicker and easier and gives a good strong line.

Cartooning different kinds of cat

Fat cat

Broad, coloured patches on a white coat help to make the cat look fat.

Very round, big face and body.

Big paws

Wide legs

Longhaired cat

Do the face and body as semi-circles.

To give the impression of long, flowing fur, do looped lines hanging from the tail and the backs of the legs.

Add tufts on the tips of the ears.

Thin cat

A curved body and tail look slinky.

Make the basic face shape like a leaf for an exotic look.

Bright blue eyes.

Colouring the legs and tail in dark grey makes them look slim and creates Siamese markings.

Kittens

Spiky whiskers give a lively look.

Short, stiff, pointed tail.

For this tabby colour, use light brown as a base. When it is dry, add the stripes in dark brown pencil, ink or felt tip.

Tiny movement lines add energy and action.

Cat characters

It is fun and good practice to try cartooning different cat characters. Below are a few to copy. Notice how you can completely alter the cat's expression and character just by changing details like the head shape.

Alley cat

A nick at the edge of one ear suggests the cat has been in a fight.

Make the whiskers bent and ragged.

A fish skeleton shows the cat has been scavenging through dustbins.

A big grin gives a jaunty air.

Put in the occasional zigzag for a scruffy look.

Sly cat

A pointed, diamond-shaped face gives a cunning air.

Slanting eyes.

Do Siamese markings.* The dark-brown "mask" makes the cat look more sinister.

A long, low body makes the cat look sneaky.

Big "wicked" grin.

Smug cat

Set the eyes high up the face so the cat seems to be looking down its nose.

Draw the eyelids half-closed.

A small, neat smile gives a smug look.

Upturned whiskers increase the snooty expression.

Pale blue shading makes the white look crisp and clean.

Scaredy cat

Zigzag ridges on the back look like raised fur.

Make the eyes wide. Add the black pupils when the yellow base is dry.

Jagged black and white patches add to the spiky, tense feel.

58   *See page 57.

Comic cat capers

When you do comic sequences like those below, keep the backgrounds fairly plain and simple, so they don't distract from what is going on in the cartoon.

Falling cat

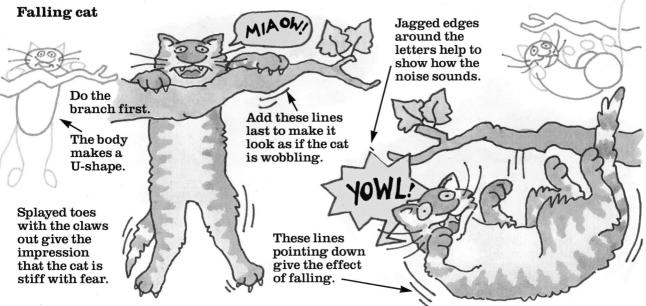

Do the branch first.

The body makes a U-shape.

MIAOW!

Add these lines last to make it look as if the cat is wobbling.

Jagged edges around the letters help to show how the noise sounds.

Splayed toes with the claws out give the impression that the cat is stiff with fear.

YOWL!

These lines pointing down give the effect of falling.

Cat in a cauldron

This strip cartoon is based on the idea that cats have nine lives and so can survive almost any mishap. Sketch out the strip in pencil, starting with the boxes. Use a ruler to make sure all the frames are even.

In each frame, do the cat first, then the main objects like the broom. Add the witch, then the sound effects and finishing touches like the movement lines, bubbles, steam and splashes of potion.

YOWL!

HEE! HEE!!

Legendary cats

Throughout history, cats have been both feared and worshipped by people all over the world. Here are a few which have made their mark.

Bast

The Ancient Egyptians were some of the first people known to have kept pet cats. They believed the animals were sacred, and worshipped a cat goddess called Bast or Bastet. She was the goddess of life and was also associated with light, music and pleasure.

Use a rich rust-red to suggest that the statue is made of clay or pottery.

Elbows on this line.

Dividing the basic L-shape roughly into thirds like this may help you get the proportions right.

Lines parallel with the front of the base help keep the kittens in perspective.

We know about Bast from old Egyptian paintings and statues like the one on the left. She was usually shown as an elegant, slim woman with a cat's head. To draw this statue, start with a three-dimensional L-shape for the basic figure. Add the head and arms as shown. Refine the outlines and fill in the details before colouring the picture.

This is a musical instrument called a sistrum.

Black cats

Colour the eyes in a brilliant copper.

Black cats are symbols of good luck in some places, but they have also been traditionally linked with witchcraft and the Devil.

Sabre-toothed tiger

This big cat, also known as Smilodon, lived millions of years ago in prehistoric times and is now extinct. It was only distantly related to the tigers of today, and in fact probably looked more like a lion. It had a massive, powerful body and huge jaws spiked with 15cm (6in) fangs to kill its prey.

Try tracing this sabre-toothed tiger, or build it up using the same basic shapes as for a lioness.*

Make the tail a bit like a lynx's.

Add the fangs last, in white.

Colour the fur tawny like a lion, with a pale belly.

This mixed view is probably because their jet-black fur and glowing eyes look especially beautiful but also a bit sinister and mysterious. To get a rich, gleaming black, use a grey, dark-blue or violet base. Leave this to show through where there are highlights. Gradually deepen the colour on the darker parts with black pencil or paint. For the blackest shadows, do the strokes very close together.

Use the tips on page 47 to help you with this position and the eerie moonlit background.

*See pages 54-55.

Making your pictures work

Good pictures involve more than just drawing convincing likenesses. Here are tips about four elements which add a lot of impact to a picture.

Composition

Roughly sketch the whole triangle first, then work out each kitten's place in it before putting in the details.

The composition of a picture means the way all the things in it are arranged. Here are two ways to group four kittens into a good composition. In the picture above, the kittens form a triangle. The grouping is interesting because the kittens look so alike but are on slightly different levels. The triangle shape draws your eye from left to right across each face.

This grouping also works well because it is nearly symmetrical: if you folded it vertically down the middle, each half would almost mirror the other.

A good way to compose a picture is to sketch each thing you want to include on a separate scrap of paper. Move the bits around until they look right together.

Point of view

The angle or point of view from which you draw can add power to a scene. This prowling kitten is seen from its own eye-level, making a dramatic picture as you look straight into its stare.

The blades of grass show how small the kitten is: its tail hardly comes above them.

Draw the kitten first. Its body is hidden because of foreshortening, so make the face detailed as it is the focus of attention. Put the grass and flowers in last.

Light and dark

Do a pale yellowy-white base for the fur, then build up the shading in tawny brown. Add the dark spots on top.

The lines of the leopard's back and tummy echo the curves of the branches above and below it.

The spots and stripes of wild cats like this leopard are not just decorative, but help to hide or camouflage them.

Light and shadow help to give shape and colour to things (see pages 37 and 40). They also add contrast and mood to a picture and stop it looking flat and dull. Here, the dappled shadows cast by the light falling through the leaves blend in with the leopard's spotted coat and make an eye-catching scene. Draw the branches and leaves first, as the leopard's position is shaped by what it is lying on. To colour the scene, first note the light source, which is sunshine from above. This and the foliage affect where you need to shade the fur.

Backgrounds

Putting a background in a picture stops the main image "floating" on the page and adds atmosphere. It can also help to focus your eye on the cat (see page 46). In this case, it brings out the cats' shapes and colours by echoing them.

For this scene, sketch in the lines of the sofa to help you judge where to put the cats. Draw them in, making them quite detailed so they stand out. Use loose blotches for the flowered pattern so it is not too distracting.

As the cats are facing left, place them slightly to the right of the picture to balance it properly.

The flowers echo the round, blooming faces of these Persian cats.

Cat outlines

These outlines were done in pen and ink. The line can vary a little in thickness, depending on how hard you press on the nib. This makes the outlines look smooth and flowing. To copy the cats, sketch the basic body shapes in pencil first. Or just trace the outlines and colour the cats in.

Part Three
HOW TO DRAW
ROBOTS AND ALIENS

Janet Cook

Edited by Judy Tatchell

Designed by Mary Forster and Nigel Reece

Illustrated by Kuo Kang Chen and Keith Hodgson

Additional illustrations by Peter Scanlan and Chris Reed

Contents

Drawing robots and aliens

These two pages tell you something about the following part of the book and about the materials you can use for drawing and colouring.

How can you tell if an alien is friendly? Pages 80-81 will give you some hints.

Find out what spaceships might look like on pages 86-87.

Can you imagine an alien rock musician? Find out how to draw this one on page 84.

Ideas for comic-strip robots and aliens are dotted about the book.

Pencils

Drawing is easier if you have the right pencil for the job. Hard pencils are good for neat edges and detail. Softer ones are good for shading.

This thin lead is good for details and outlines.

This is good for general drawing.

This is good for shading small areas neatly.

Use this soft lead to shade large areas.

You can tell how hard a pencil is by looking at the marking on its side. H stands for hard, and B stands for black, which means the pencil has a soft lead.

Paper

For sketches, any scrap paper will do, but for a really professional look, it is a good idea to invest in some art paper. Here are some types to look for. A good art shop will also give you advice.

Watercolour paper

This paper takes paint well. There is a wide range of textures to choose from. The smoothest paper is good for detailed work. Bumpy paper is better for loose, wispy effects.

Cartridge paper and Bristol board

These are even less textured than the smoothest watercolour paper. They are good choices when you are using wax or pencil crayons, but paint tends to run on them.

One step at a time...

Most of the drawings in the book are broken down into two or three stages for you to follow. For example, the diagrams below show how to draw a spaceship.

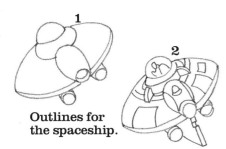

Outlines for the spaceship.

Always draw the lines shown in green first, then the red ones. Remember to erase any lines that are not on the finished image.

Colouring materials

There are lots of different materials you can choose from to colour your pictures. Here are some of them.

Drawing inks can be applied with a brush or an ink pen. They are good for details.

Gouache paints give you a stronger, flatter look than watercolours.

How to stop paper from wrinkling

When you paint, paper gets wet and stretches slightly. Then as it dries, it shrinks. This can cause watercolour paper to wrinkle. To prevent this from happening, you can stretch the paper before you paint on it.

1. Position the paper on some board. Use a brush or sponge to wet it all over with clean water.

2. Smooth the paper flat, then tape it to the board. Let it dry, then remove it from the board.

Tape down all four sides.

You can buy pre-stretched paper, or thick paper that does not need stretching. However, it is usually quite expensive.

Pastels are like soft sticks of chalk. They blend together smoothly, but are too thick for detailed work.

Watercolour paints are useful for creating texture, or for a subtle, delicate look.

Pencil crayons come in many colours. You use the tip for details, and the side for shading.

Poster paints are similar to gouache. Although cheaper, there are not as many colours.

Thick wax crayons are good for large areas. They leave a shiny finish.

First robots

You can get ideas for drawing robots by looking at everyday objects and making them come alive. The robots below have tin cans for their bodies.

They have been painted with a specialist artists' tool known as an airbrush. You can achieve a similar effect with paints.

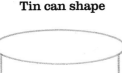

Tin can shape

A curved window makes the robot look rounded.

The lines shown by dashes are not on the finished picture.

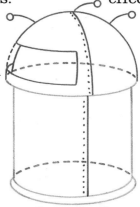

These circles are meant to be lights.

1. Using your pencil, copy this tin can shape. To make the sides really straight, use a ruler or the side of a book.

2. Draw a dome for the head. Add an eye window, antennae, a seam line and some tiny bolts. Erase the lines shown by dashes.

3. Now draw some rectangles and circles on the robot's body. Add two more lines and a row of bolts on its head.

Pincer

Go over the whole outline in thin black felt tip.

Pale patches look like shiny metal.

Leave part of each light white.

You can find out more about how to make things shiny on pages 72-73.

Dark colour for shadow.

Add a grey area beneath the wheel to make the robot stand on the ground.

4. Draw two tubes for each arm, then add circular shapes for the shoulders, elbows and wrists. Now add some pincers.

5. Finally, add a base and two wheels under the robot.

More tin can robots

Now that you can draw a robot's body, the possibilities are endless. Below are some more tin can robots. First copy the green lines, then add the red ones. You could then try inventing some robots with tin can bodies yourself.

1

Erase any extra lines, like this one.

A groove makes the head look 3-D.

2

3

Robot malfunction

This robot has lost control. Use felt tips or pencil crayons to colour it in.

Thin, straight lines show parts bursting off.

Curly lines for wire springs.

Dots add to the confusion.

Solid knobs instead of pincers.

1

3

Thick tread

Invent a control panel.

Because there is hardly any shading, this cartoon robot looks quite flat.

2

Correcting mistakes

If you make a mistake when you are drawing, erase it carefully. Lots of gentle motions are less likely to scuff paper than a few firm ones.

Cut the end off your eraser if it is dirty.

1

The body is wider at the top.

3

Suction cup

2

Make it walk towards you.

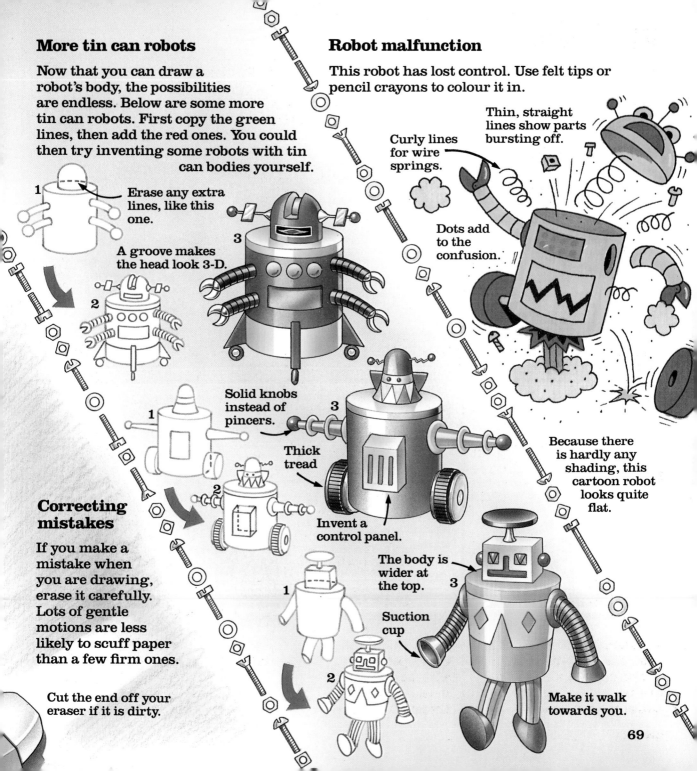

69

More difficult robots

You can make impressive robots out of geometric shapes. Here is an octagonal (eight-sided) robot, and a more rounded one. They have been painted to look quite realistic, with shadows and highlights to give them shape.

The animal robots opposite are coloured in a simpler, flatter style. This style is more suitable for cartoons.

The tips below will help you to achieve a good finish with poster paints or watercolours.

Painting tips

- Use several thin layers of paint, rather than one thick layer.

- For a crisp finish, let the paint dry between layers.

- For a soft look, add each new layer while the previous one is still slightly damp.

- Once the final layer is dry, you can add highlights and touch up shadows with pencil crayons.

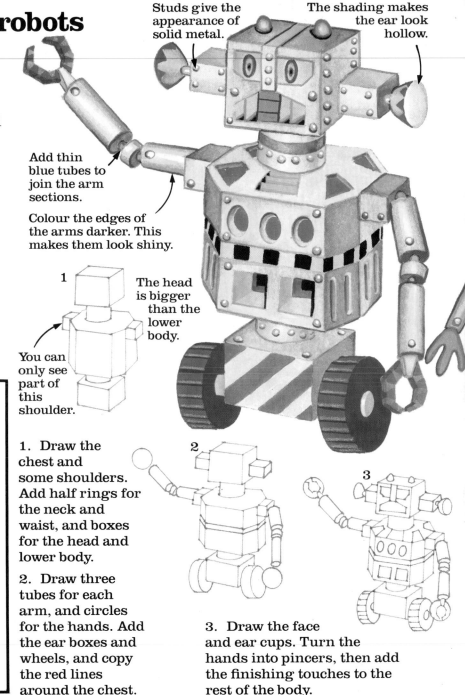

Studs give the appearance of solid metal.

The shading makes the ear look hollow.

Add thin blue tubes to join the arm sections.

Colour the edges of the arms darker. This makes them look shiny.

1

The head is bigger than the lower body.

You can only see part of this shoulder.

1. Draw the chest and some shoulders. Add half rings for the neck and waist, and boxes for the head and lower body.

2. Draw three tubes for each arm, and circles for the hands. Add the ear boxes and wheels, and copy the red lines around the chest.

2

3

3. Draw the face and ear cups. Turn the hands into pincers, then add the finishing touches to the rest of the body.

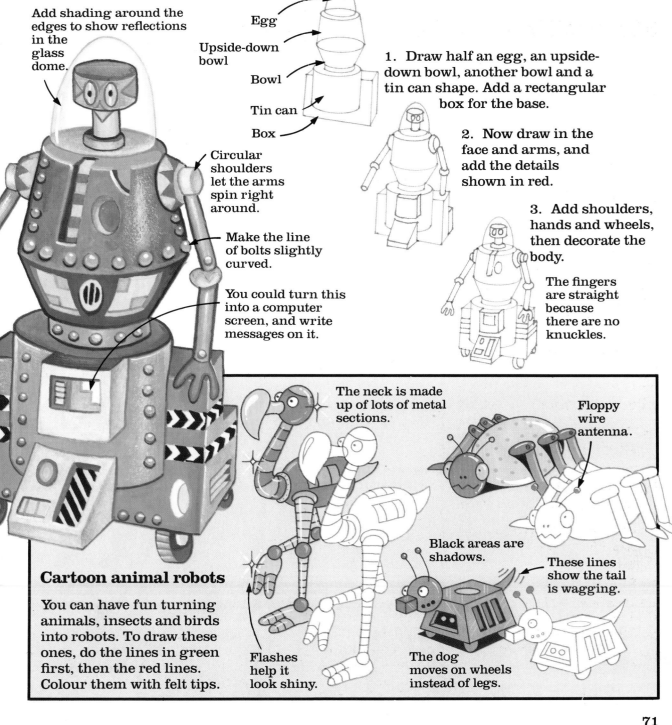

Add shading around the edges to show reflections in the glass dome.

Egg

Upside-down bowl

Bowl

Tin can

Box

1. Draw half an egg, an upside-down bowl, another bowl and a tin can shape. Add a rectangular box for the base.

2. Now draw in the face and arms, and add the details shown in red.

3. Add shoulders, hands and wheels, then decorate the body.

The fingers are straight because there are no knuckles.

Circular shoulders let the arms spin right around.

Make the line of bolts slightly curved.

You could turn this into a computer screen, and write messages on it.

The neck is made up of lots of metal sections.

Floppy wire antenna.

Black areas are shadows.

These lines show the tail is wagging.

Cartoon animal robots

You can have fun turning animals, insects and birds into robots. To draw these ones, do the lines in green first, then the red lines. Colour them with felt tips.

Flashes help it look shiny.

The dog moves on wheels instead of legs.

71

Androids

Many of the robots you see in science fiction movies look like human beings. These are called androids. Below you can find out how to draw and paint a really hi-tech android. There are also some cartoon androids for fun.

Drawing your android

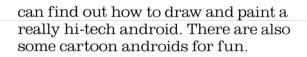

1. **Start with this outline. Press gently so you can erase it later.**

2. **Now make the robot more solid. Erase any hidden green lines.**

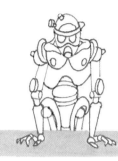

3. **Add the blue lines to give it joints and pull it together.**

Preparing a palette

First choose the colour you want to use for the android. Mix white paint with it in the amounts shown below so that you end up with four shades plus pure white.

1. Pure green

2. ³/₄ green ¹/₄ white

3. ¹/₂ green ¹/₂ white

4. ¹/₄ green ³/₄ white

5. Pure white

Painting your android

Before starting, you have to decide which direction you want the light to come from. You will then know which areas are shady and which are bright. Here, it is coming from the right.

1. Take your darkest shade and paint the areas on the robot which would not catch any light.

2. Paint a strip alongside the area you have just painted, using the second darkest shade.

For a bold look, colour the robot in gouache or poster paint.

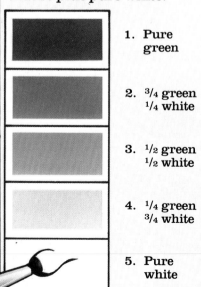

This is hidden from the light.

Light comes from this direction.

Use lines (hatching) or dots (stippling) to blend the colours.

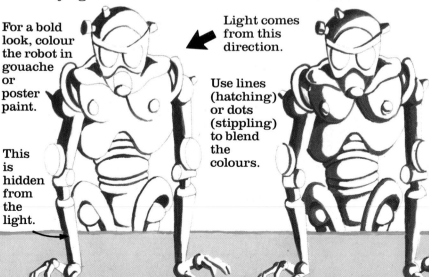

72

Cartoon androids

You can have great fun turning people into robots. Here are a couple to start you off. Remember to draw the outlines in pencil so you can erase them.

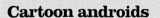

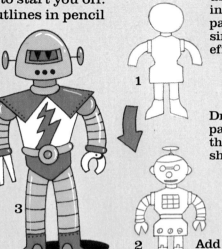

1

A black outline makes it stand out.

White streaks make it shiny.

Curved lines make the arms and legs seem rounded.

2

3

You could use felt tips instead of paint for a similar effect.

1

3

Draw a black patch for the robot's shadow.

2 Add shoelaces.

5. Add white crayon to the middle of the light areas. Don't overdo it, or you will lose the shiny effect.

Let some paint show through.

3. Fill in the rest of the figure with shade 3. Add white paint to any parts you want to stand out.

Shade 3

Let the paint dry before adding shade 4.

4. Now take shade 4 and paint the areas that the light hits, blending the colours as before.

Shade 4

Vary the pressure on your pencil crayon.

Hatching

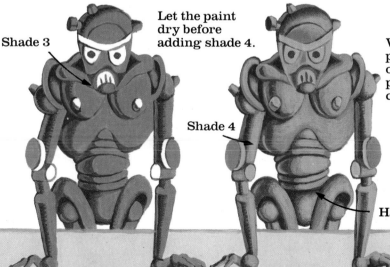

Transformers®

Some robots can turn into other things such as cars. These are called Transformers®. Parts such as wheels are cleverly disguised on the robots' bodies so you would never guess they had other uses. Here, one robot is turning into a racing car and another, into a rocket.

Racing car Transformer®

This Transformer® looks very tricky. If you copy the outlines one step at a time, though, you will end up with a very impressive series of pictures. Use a fairly hard pencil (see page 66).

1. Draw the robot's head and torso, then add the arms and legs.

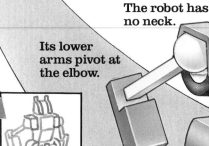

2. Add the parts shown here in red.

3. Draw in the face and add details to the body.

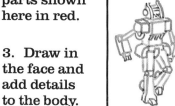

The robot has no neck.

Its lower arms pivot at the elbow.

Could these be wheels?

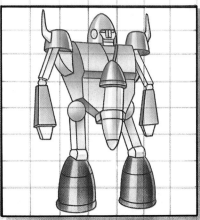

Rocket Transformer®

One way to copy shapes is to use a grid. Usually, you first need to draw a grid on tracing paper and lay it over the picture, but here it has been drawn for you.

1. Draw another grid with the same number of squares as the grid over the main picture. For a large picture, make the squares big.

2. Now look closely at the picture. Copy the shape inside each square until you have drawn the whole robot. Erase the squares.

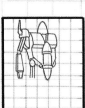

The robot's wide chest will form the middle of the rocket.

The robot's pointed body disguises the rocket's nose.

Enormous feet hide the rocket's engines.

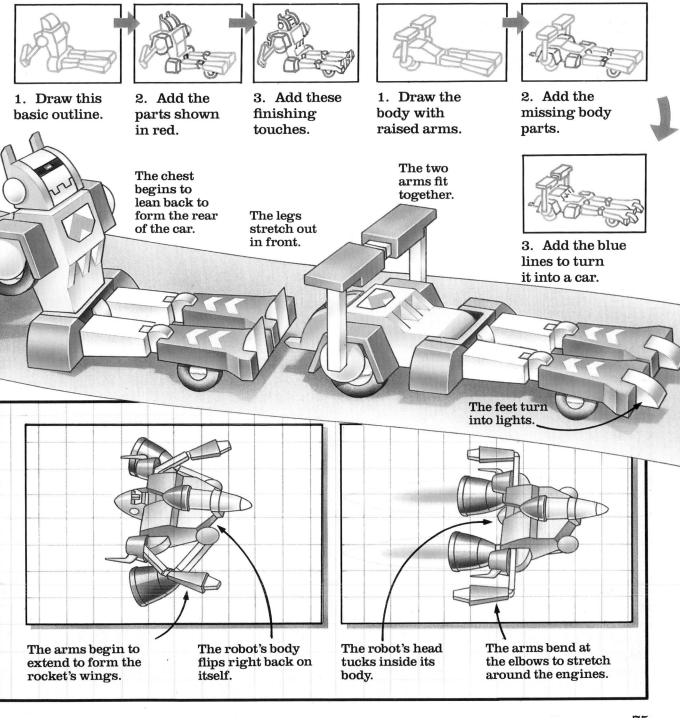

1. Draw this basic outline.

2. Add the parts shown in red.

3. Add these finishing touches.

1. Draw the body with raised arms.

2. Add the missing body parts.

3. Add the blue lines to turn it into a car.

The chest begins to lean back to form the rear of the car.

The legs stretch out in front.

The two arms fit together.

The feet turn into lights.

The arms begin to extend to form the rocket's wings.

The robot's body flips right back on itself.

The robot's head tucks inside its body.

The arms bend at the elbows to stretch around the engines.

Useful robots

Imagine having no more chores. Instead, you would just program your robot to do them for you . . .

Below are a number of robots at work. You could also invent robots suited to your least favourite task.

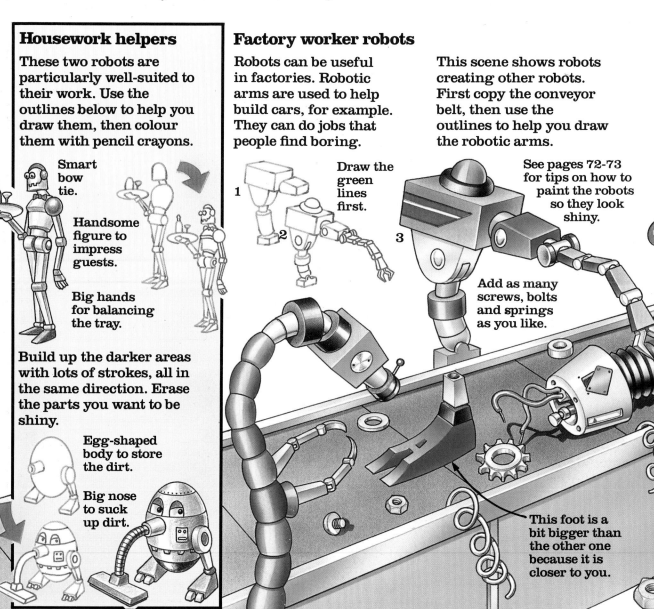

Housework helpers

These two robots are particularly well-suited to their work. Use the outlines below to help you draw them, then colour them with pencil crayons.

Smart bow tie.

Handsome figure to impress guests.

Big hands for balancing the tray.

Build up the darker areas with lots of strokes, all in the same direction. Erase the parts you want to be shiny.

Egg-shaped body to store the dirt.

Big nose to suck up dirt.

Factory worker robots

Robots can be useful in factories. Robotic arms are used to help build cars, for example. They can do jobs that people find boring.

This scene shows robots creating other robots. First copy the conveyor belt, then use the outlines to help you draw the robotic arms.

1

Draw the green lines first.

2

3

See pages 72-73 for tips on how to paint the robots so they look shiny.

Add as many screws, bolts and springs as you like.

This foot is a bit bigger than the other one because it is closer to you.

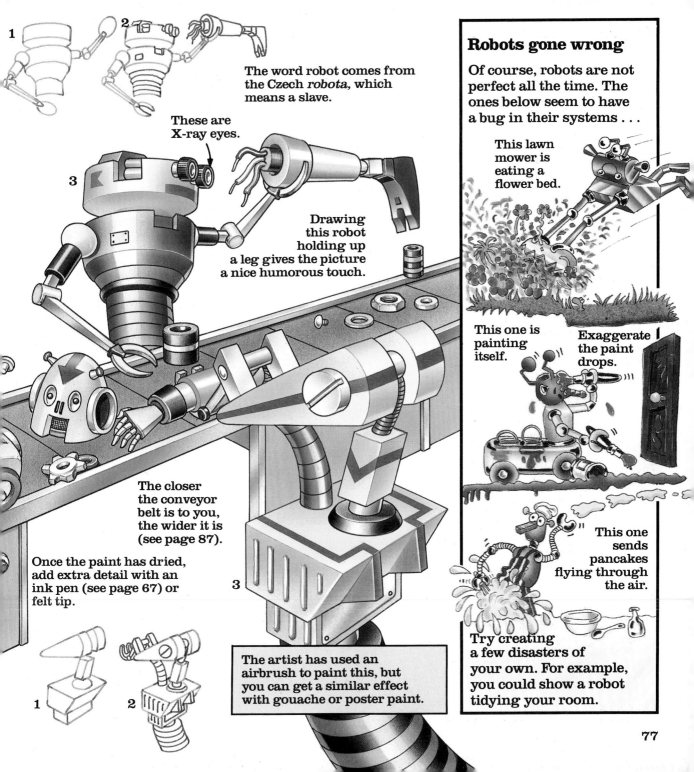

1

2

The word robot comes from the Czech *robota*, which means a slave.

These are X-ray eyes.

3

Drawing this robot holding up a leg gives the picture a nice humorous touch.

The closer the conveyor belt is to you, the wider it is (see page 87).

Once the paint has dried, add extra detail with an ink pen (see page 67) or felt tip.

3

1

2

The artist has used an airbrush to paint this, but you can get a similar effect with gouache or poster paint.

Robots gone wrong

Of course, robots are not perfect all the time. The ones below seem to have a bug in their systems . . .

This lawn mower is eating a flower bed.

This one is painting itself.

Exaggerate the paint drops.

This one sends pancakes flying through the air.

Try creating a few disasters of your own. For example, you could show a robot tidying your room.

First aliens

The aliens on these two pages are quite simple. All you have to do is draw a few circular shapes, and you are halfway there . . .

Goofy alien

1. Draw two large ovals, overlapping each other. Add circles for the joints and hands, then draw sticks for the limbs.

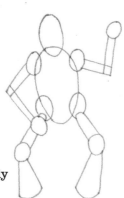

The legs gradually get wider.

You need two shades of each colour, one light and one dark.

See the other ideas for eyes on the left.

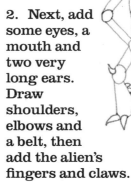

2. Next, add some eyes, a mouth and two very long ears. Draw shoulders, elbows and a belt, then add the alien's fingers and claws.

3. Now copy the lines shown in blue to add some extra details to the alien's clothes and body. Finally, colour her in with crayons, following the tips on the right.

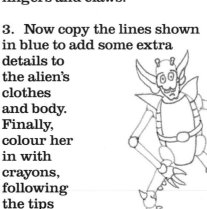

Alien eyes

You can change your alien's mood by just adding a couple of lines to her eyes.

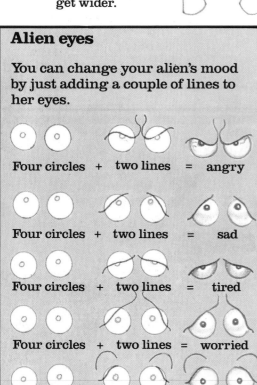

Four circles + two lines = angry

Four circles + two lines = sad

Four circles + two lines = tired

Four circles + two lines = worried

Four circles + four lines = surprised

78

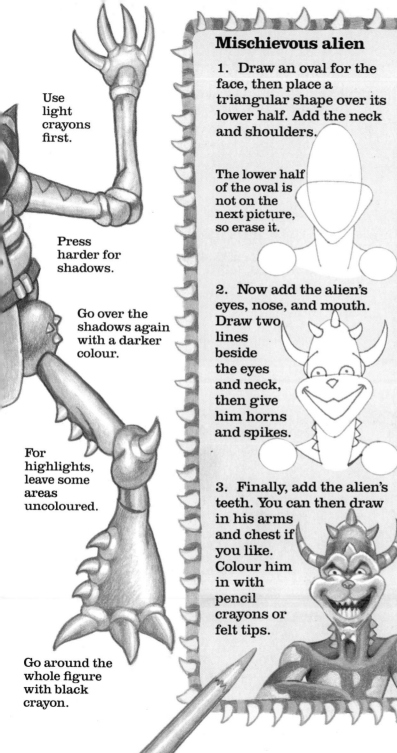

Use light crayons first.

Press harder for shadows.

Go over the shadows again with a darker colour.

For highlights, leave some areas uncoloured.

Go around the whole figure with black crayon.

Mischievous alien

1. Draw an oval for the face, then place a triangular shape over its lower half. Add the neck and shoulders.

The lower half of the oval is not on the next picture, so erase it.

2. Now add the alien's eyes, nose, and mouth. Draw two lines beside the eyes and neck, then give him horns and spikes.

3. Finally, add the alien's teeth. You can then draw in his arms and chest if you like. Colour him in with pencil crayons or felt tips.

Alien friends

You can have a lot of fun turning your friends into aliens. Start by drawing a caricature.

Carrot-top hair

Sticking-out ears

Long chin

A caricature, such as the picture above, exaggerates someone's main features.

Now draw an alien with these features, exaggerated even further and coloured in an extraordinary, alien way.

Antenna

Extended forehead

Enormous ears

Extra-long chin

Blue and orange colouring

Here are a few other people with their alien counterparts.

Friend or foe?

How do you make an alien look friendly? A smile is not enough: he may be contemplating his next meal – you. For example, look at the portraits of the four aliens on these pages. Two of them may be friendly, the others are not. Before reading the words, decide which ones are your enemies.

Deceptive appearances

This cartoon alien seems too small to harm you. But wait . . .

Here, she has one circle for her neck.

Now she has two.

Now it is fully extended.

Vultawk

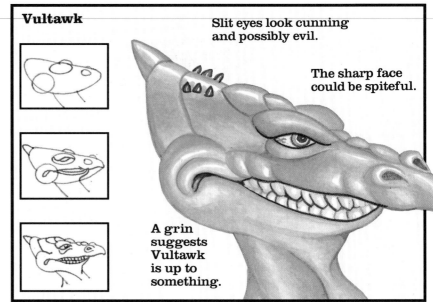

Slit eyes look cunning and possibly evil.

The sharp face could be spiteful.

A grin suggests Vultawk is up to something.

Lord Hydlebar

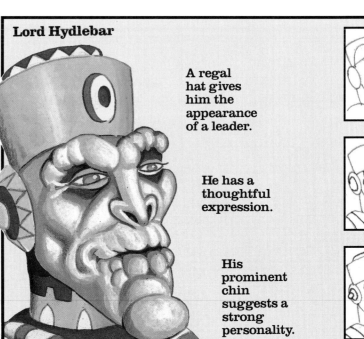

A regal hat gives him the appearance of a leader.

He has a thoughtful expression.

His prominent chin suggests a strong personality.

Solero

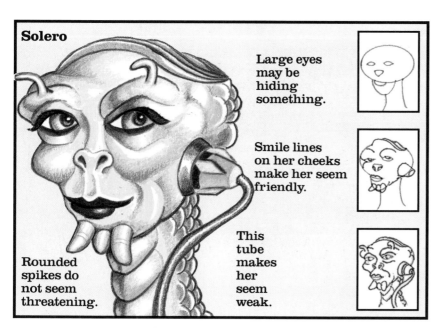

Large eyes may be hiding something.

Smile lines on her cheeks make her seem friendly.

This tube makes her seem weak.

Rounded spikes do not seem threatening.

Drummader

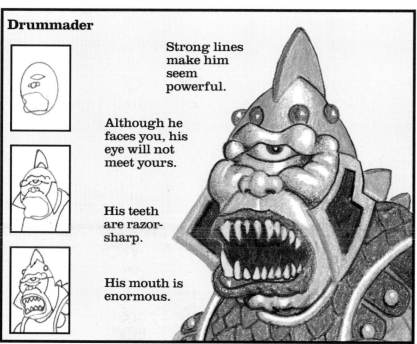

Strong lines make him seem powerful.

Although he faces you, his eye will not meet yours.

His teeth are razor-sharp.

His mouth is enormous.

Colouring the aliens

Choosing what you will colour each alien with is very important. Here, you can see why.

Watercolours are good for making Vultawk's skin seem very smooth. This helps to give him a cold, slippery look.

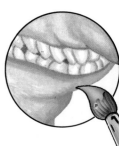

Gouache makes Lord Hydlebar look slick. Leave a dark gap between his lips to show he has no teeth.

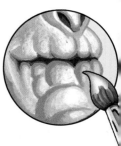

Pencil crayon gives Solero soft edges to make her look gentle. Lots of dark curves on her neck look like warts.

Use wax crayons for Drummader's leathery skin and rough armour. White highlights make his skin look sweaty.

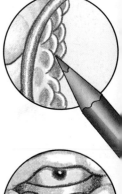

Aliens on the move

How do aliens get around? Some might dart or leap, others might slither along in their slime. Some lucky aliens might even have space buggies.

These aliens were coloured using an airbrush. You can also get good results with watercolours and crayons. For instance, follow the tips on the right to colour the alien below.

True slime

First paint the darker areas with a layer of deep greeny-blue watercolour. Let the paint dry, then go over the whole body with a lighter shade. Now touch up the shady areas again with the darker colour. Add small dabs of white paint to look like light glistening on the alien's wet skin.

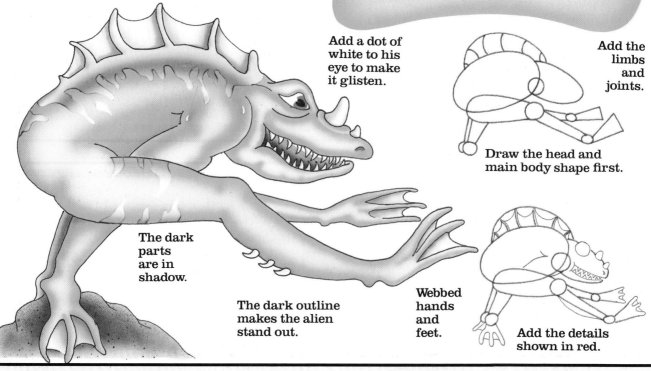

Add a dot of white to his eye to make it glisten.

Add the limbs and joints.

Draw the head and main body shape first.

The dark parts are in shadow.

The dark outline makes the alien stand out.

Webbed hands and feet.

Add the details shown in red.

Fast-action wall frieze

For this frieze, use the outlines for the alien above but change the position of each body part as he moves.

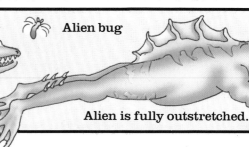

Alien bug

Alien is fully outstretched.

Creepy-crawly alien

Draw this alien using the two outlines below to help you get the shape right. Go around the alien in brown pencil crayon, then colour her in.

Circles for the joints.

Three tubes for each leg.

Your alien could be a different colour.

Make pointed feet as shown in red.

Make the hairs look ragged.

First paint a layer of pale watercolour over the body. Let it dry, then add shading in pencil crayon, in a deeper colour. Draw dark hairs on top. Bald patches and tufts of hair look creepier than hair all over.

Alien space buggy

Construct this space buggy one shape at a time, using the outlines on the far right. Add the alien last of all.

You can colour the buggy with watercolour or poster paint. You could then put some mounds or craters in the background.

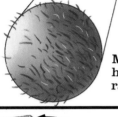

Start by drawing the boxes.

Add the circular shapes.

Erase the extra lines.

Thick grooves help the buggy travel across rough ground.

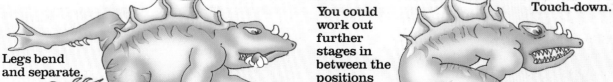

Legs bend and separate.

You could work out further stages in between the positions shown here.

Touch-down.

Aliens at play

What do you think aliens would do for fun? Play sports? Watch television? Go to the movies or a rock concert?

These pictures show some rather unusual rock musicians and an equally weird fan. The artist coloured them using an airbrush. You could colour yours by putting down several flat layers of watercolour or coloured ink. When these are dry, add shading with pencil crayons. For a slightly paler look, just use pencil crayons.

White patches make this bald head look shiny.

Soft-edged highlights make the alien's body look rounded.

Singer

1. As you can see, the singer's outline is mostly made up of rounded shapes.

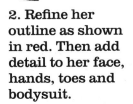

A white highlight makes the eyes come alive.

Hard-edged, streaky highlights make the guitar look hard and flat.

2. Refine her outline as shown in red. Then add detail to her face, hands, toes and bodysuit.

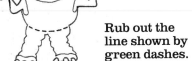

Rub out the line shown by green dashes.

Guitarist

1. Sketch the alien's body shapes, then the guitar.

2. Refine the outline and add more detail as shown in red.

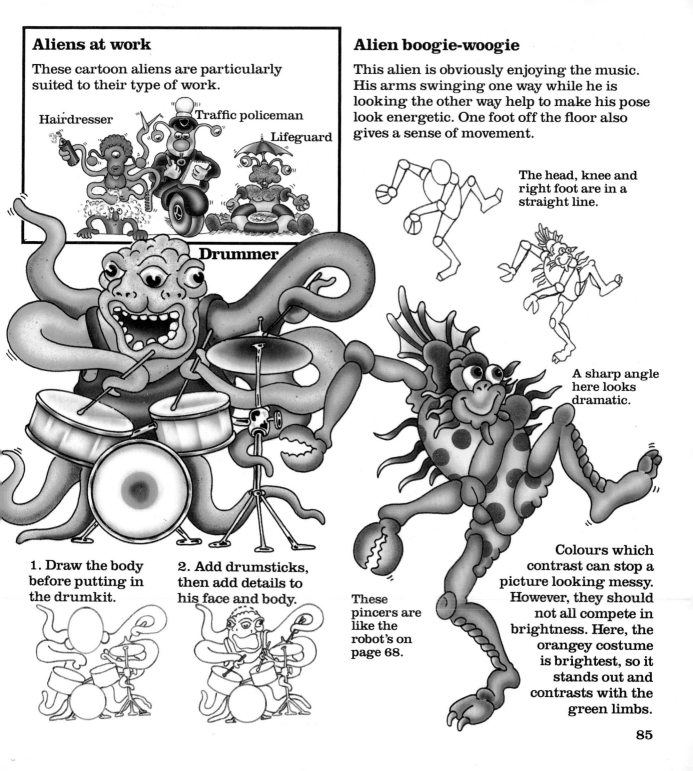

Aliens at work

These cartoon aliens are particularly suited to their type of work.

Hairdresser

Traffic policeman

Lifeguard

Drummer

1. Draw the body before putting in the drumkit.

2. Add drumsticks, then add details to his face and body.

Alien boogie-woogie

This alien is obviously enjoying the music. His arms swinging one way while he is looking the other way help to make his pose look energetic. One foot off the floor also gives a sense of movement.

The head, knee and right foot are in a straight line.

A sharp angle here looks dramatic.

These pincers are like the robot's on page 68.

Colours which contrast can stop a picture looking messy. However, they should not all compete in brightness. Here, the orangey costume is brightest, so it stands out and contrasts with the green limbs.

85

Spaceships

What do spaceships look like? It may depend on what they are designed for. For instance, a police spaceship would need to be fast, whereas it would be more important for a family spaceship to be comfortable.

The spaceships on these two pages are airbrushed, which gives them a very smooth finish. You could use poster paints for a bold effect.

Police spaceship

This spaceship is designed for the alien police force. Its saucer shape enables it to do quick U-turns, and the revolving chair and circular glass dome give the pilot all-round vision. It has three powerful engines for speedy chases.

White highlights follow the spaceship's curves. Their hard edges make the surface look smooth.

Pale blue edges look like reflections in the glass dome.

Taking off and landing

These cartoon spaceships are about to launch or to land. How do you think the three large spaceships on these pages might take off or land? You could draw them in action.

This flying saucer is thrust upwards by lots of thin jets of water.

This is propelled by a launching pad that works like a trampoline.

The spaceship below lands by dropping down massive feet.

Paint white highlights along this edge.

To blend tones, add the second colour while the first is still damp.

Draw the main body, then the engines.

Add an alien and details to the ship.

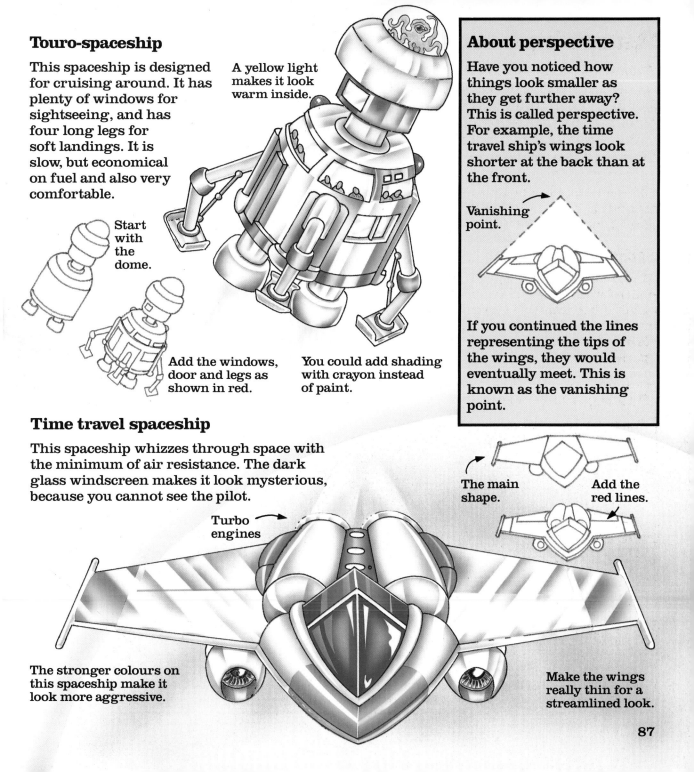

Touro-spaceship

This spaceship is designed for cruising around. It has plenty of windows for sightseeing, and has four long legs for soft landings. It is slow, but economical on fuel and also very comfortable.

A yellow light makes it look warm inside.

Start with the dome.

Add the windows, door and legs as shown in red.

You could add shading with crayon instead of paint.

About perspective

Have you noticed how things look smaller as they get further away? This is called perspective. For example, the time travel ship's wings look shorter at the back than at the front.

Vanishing point.

If you continued the lines representing the tips of the wings, they would eventually meet. This is known as the vanishing point.

Time travel spaceship

This spaceship whizzes through space with the minimum of air resistance. The dark glass windscreen makes it look mysterious, because you cannot see the pilot.

Turbo engines

The main shape.

Add the red lines.

The stronger colours on this spaceship make it look more aggressive.

Make the wings really thin for a streamlined look.

Aliens on Earth

How would you react if you saw an alien spaceship landing on the street? What would an alien think of you and your planet? Here are a few ideas . . .

Drawing the spaceship

1. Start by drawing an upside-down hat, then add some curved lines. Draw the aliens, starting with their heads, then their chests and arms.

2. Show the aliens' faces inside the helmets. Draw in their spacesuits, then add fins and stabilizers to the ship. Now give the aliens some fingers.

3. Add lights and more stabilizers, then draw tubes coming out of the helmets. Finally, add the finishing touches to the aliens shown in blue.

Use paint to make the sky really flat.

Use wax crayon for the larger areas.

The aliens' faces are coloured with pencil crayon.

Keep the background uncluttered so the ship stands out.

Use purple for the shady parts of the ship, red next to this, then pink where light hits.

Comic strips

A comic strip is a fun way to tell a story. This strip is about a group of aliens landing on Earth. Around it are tips to help you create your own strip. Strong, fairly flat colours look good in comic strips.

Sounds help it come to life.

A short caption sets the scene.

The different frame shapes add interest.

A FLYING SAUCER BLASTS THROUGH SPACE TOWARDS . . . EARTH!

VAROOM

EARTH

TOUCHDOWN!

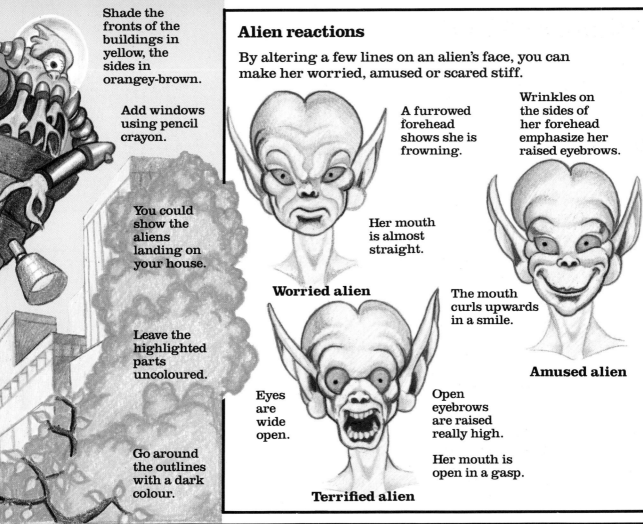

Shade the fronts of the buildings in yellow, the sides in orangey-brown.

Add windows using pencil crayon.

You could show the aliens landing on your house.

Leave the highlighted parts uncoloured.

Go around the outlines with a dark colour.

Alien reactions

By altering a few lines on an alien's face, you can make her worried, amused or scared stiff.

A furrowed forehead shows she is frowning.

Wrinkles on the sides of her forehead emphasize her raised eyebrows.

Her mouth is almost straight.

Worried alien

The mouth curls upwards in a smile.

Amused alien

Eyes are wide open.

Open eyebrows are raised really high.

Her mouth is open in a gasp.

Terrified alien

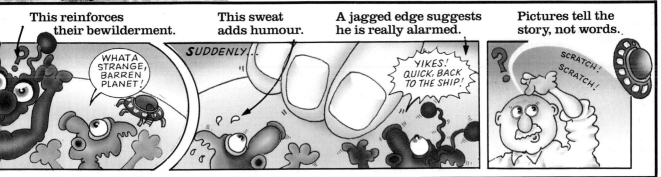

This reinforces their bewilderment.

This sweat adds humour.

A jagged edge suggests he is really alarmed.

Pictures tell the story, not words.

WHAT A STRANGE, BARREN PLANET!

SUDDENLY...

YIKES! QUICK, BACK TO THE SHIP!

SCRATCH! SCRATCH!

An alien town

You can have fun dreaming up ideas for a town in outer space. This scene will start you off. You might also like to add things from elsewhere in the book.

Instead of copying the outlines, you could use the grid method described on page 74. You will first need to draw a grid on tracing paper and tape it to the picture.

on page 74

Monorail

1. Draw three lines for the track, then add the coaches and pylons. Draw a tunnel entrance.

2. Decorate the coaches and the tunnel, then continue the monorail track in the distance.

Barber's shop

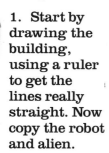

1. Start by drawing the building, using a ruler to get the lines really straight. Now copy the robot and alien.

2. Give the alien a shaggy coat, dress the robot and fill in his face. Now add the details to the chair, pipes and building.

BARBER

Paint blue and grey streaks across the barber's window.

Vanishing point (see page 87).

Things become less distinct the further away they are.

Space helmets filter out poisonous gases.

The ground is so smooth and clean that it looks unreal.

Alien plants

1. Draw a tall tin can with a circle in one corner. Add spiral rings around it.

2. Erase the can, then add branches, fruit and thorns to the tree.

Here are some alien flowers. You could add them to your picture.

To make this plant look really sci-fi, add highlights so it shines.

Paint masses of dark thorns on the fruit. Add white streaks to them.

For a tongue-in-cheek effect, show robots and aliens doing things humans might do in real life.

This curved door looks weird.

You could replace this spaceship with one from pages 86-87.

A robot's house

1. Draw a hut shape for the ground floor, then add the second floor. Now draw in the satellite dish.

2. Next, draw some circles between the floors, then add a door. Position an aerial on the satellite dish, then add some curved lines on the roof.

3. Draw the windows and curtains. You could add a robot waving from one of the windows. Finally, add some pipes to connect the circles.

Robots on the movie screen

Have you ever wondered how the robots that you see in films and on television are created? These two pages show their journey from just names in a script to the amazing creatures you see on-screen.

Drawing the robot

First, the director gives the script to a team that specializes in creating robots. They talk over their ideas for how the robot should look with an artist. The artist then starts work on the drawings.

The team discusses what they like or dislike about the drawings. For example, should it be cuter? Taller? More aggressive? The artist produces something everyone is happy with.

Here are three drawings by Syd Mead for the robot "Number Five" in the movie *Short Circuit.**

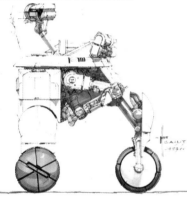

The designs above and below are less appealing than the robot shown on the right.

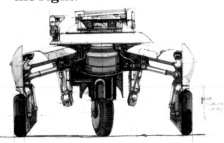

The final drawing. Small changes were later made as the robot was being built.

A laser on one side gives the robot a lop-sided appeal.

A spindly body shows the audience that no actor is hiding inside.

This lies flat when Number Five needs to crouch down and hide.

Batteries hide in here.

A tread system gives Number Five a military look (in the movie, he was originally built to fight wars).

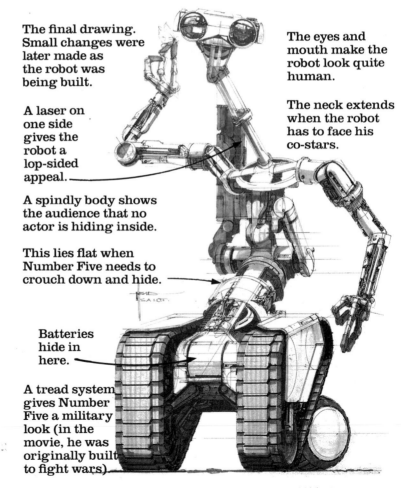

The eyes and mouth make the robot look quite human.

The neck extends when the robot has to face his co-stars.

Making a 3-D model

The team creates a model like the one on the right. They discuss the tasks it will perform. Electrical and mechanical engineers draw blueprints (designs) to show how gears and so on work.

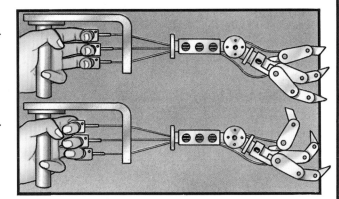

3-D model of Number Five.

The model is made out of basic materials such as paper, plastic and wood.

Building the robot

Working from the blueprints, technicians now build some of the more complicated parts of the robot. They show the film director how the eyes will move, the head tilt and so on.

If you pull ▶ on these three cables . . .

. . . Number ▶ Five's fingers will start to move.

Finally, they build a number of identical finished robots so that filming will not be held up if one breaks down. For *Short Circuit*, there were 15 identical models of Number Five.

This is Number Five with the man in charge of designing him, Eric Allard. Eric is wearing a radio-controlled device known as an upper-body telemetry suit. When he moves his arms or chest, Number Five moves in the same way.

On the set

Although some of the manoeuvres you see on-screen are performed by a radio-controlled robot, many of the close-up ones are done by puppeteers working a robot puppet.

Actress Ally Sheedy rehearsing a scene with a Number Five puppet. The television screens give the puppeteers live footage of the robot's movements.

A radio-controlled Number Five practising going up and down steps.

Mix and match

Here is an assortment of heads, chests and legs for you to mix and match. Also, here you can find some further ideas for space vehicle outlines.

The shapes at the top and bottom of the opposite page might inspire you when constructing robots and aliens from your own imagination. The robot pieces can help when drawing things from odd angles, too.

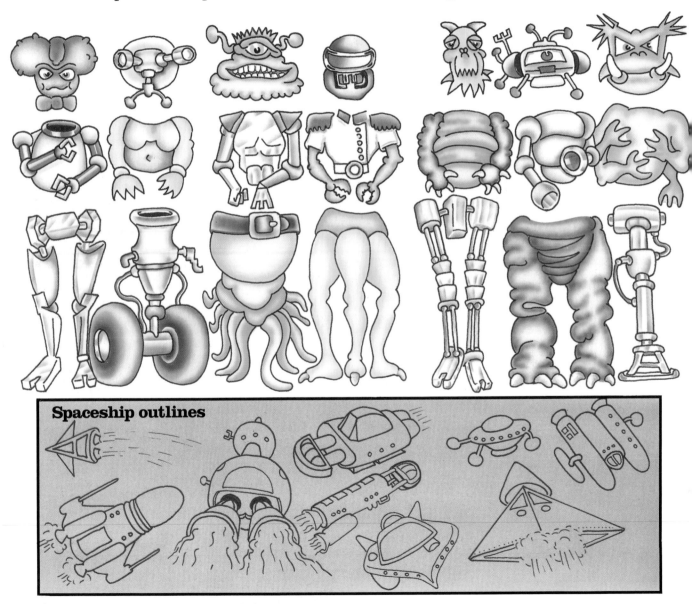

Spaceship outlines

Alien shapes

Space buggy outlines

Robot pieces

Robot inspiration

The first six of these drawings were inspired by everyday machinery and equipment. The robot animals at the bottom might give you some ideas for how to mechanize things from the natural world, as well.

Hotdog seller

Drinks machine

Ice cream seller

Road sweeper

Dust cart

Fire engine

Lion

Fish

Walrus

Part Four

HOW TO DRAW
BUILDINGS

Pam Beasant

Edited by Judy Tatchell

Designed by Iain Ashman

**Illustrated by
Iain Ashman, Isobel Gardner,
Chris Lyon and Chris Smedley**

Contents

Consultant: Iain Ashman

Consultant architect: Peter Reed

About drawing buildings

There are all sorts of exciting buildings for you to draw in this book, ranging from a cathedral to a space station. Clear, step-by-step instructions show you how to build up your pictures in stages.

Basic drawing and colouring skills and styles are introduced with many professional hints and techniques.

For instance, you can find out about perspective on page 103 and composition on page 114. Throughout the book there are tips on how to add convincing details such as shadows and highlights.

On pages 122-123, you can learn the basics of technical drawing and how to plan, draw and build your own model house.

There is a round-up of techniques and drawing tools (such as pencils and paints) on pages 126-127, to help you choose your equipment.

Drawing styles

The drawings in this book are done in various styles. Some of the main ones are shown here.

Pen and ink

Ink colour washes (see ▶ below) are added over line drawings to create shadows, highlights and graded areas of colour.

Try this pen and ink haunted house on pages 106-107.

Once you build up confidence, you can have fun experimenting with any style you choose.

Line drawings

◀ Line drawings are done with pen or pencil. You use lines or dots to give an impression of shadow. You can find out more about line drawing technique on page 111.

Washes

A wash is a thin coat of watery paint or ink. It gives a subtle, overall colour to a drawing. You can add more layers for areas of stronger colour or shadow. You can also mix and blend different coloured washes on the same drawing. (Before using a wash, see page 127 for how to stretch paper.)

Line drawing.

First layer of wash.

There is a comic book style future city on pages 116-117.

"Impressionism"

A looser style, giving an atmospheric impression of a scene, can be achieved by blending soft lines and colours.
▼

Find out more about this style on pages 120-121.

Comic book style ▲

Comic book style uses bold, black lines and deep colours. It is dramatic and can have a lot of movement.

There are skyscrapers to draw on pages 112-113.

Airbrush

◀ The smooth, flat, airbrush style is often used for modern or futuristic subjects such as skyscrapers or space cities.

There is a cartoon castle to draw on page 104.

Cartoons

◀ A cartoon style can add character and a sense of fun to a drawing. It exaggerates and changes some aspects of the subject to make it funny.

Darker colour for shadow.

Finished picture.

The first layer of wash should be very weak and watery. Then add more paint to the wash mixture to make it a darker, more concentrated shade. Apply each further layer when the last is dry. In this way, you can gradually build up contrasting areas of light and dark.

For most of the drawings in this book, you can use any colouring tools you choose, such as felt tips. You need not stick to the tools and techniques used by this book's illustrators if you do not want to.

Looking at buildings

It is a good idea to carry a small sketchbook with you when you go out for a walk. You can make quick sketches of any interesting buildings or details that you see. You can use these sketches later to invent your own drawings of buildings. You could use photographs instead, although sketching helps you to see how buildings are put together.

How buildings fit together

Sketching real buildings is the best way to see how they fit together, and how their details vary. You could try a street or a row of shop-fronts.

You can concentrate on one building in a scene. Draw just the shadowy outline of the others to frame it.

Windows and doors

Try sketching a variety of windows and doors on one page. This is a good way to compare and contrast details and experiment with sketching.

Fit as many details as you can on to one page.

Note how the shades are paler, the further away the buildings are.

A quick, loose sketch.

You can write small notes on your sketch about colour, detail and texture.

A tight, finished sketch.

Sketching a near skyline is good practice for perspective drawing.

Skylines

A skyline is often needed for background in a drawing, or to give it depth. Sketching one is a good way to see the overall shape of a city.

Painting your sketches

If you take a small paintbox and a sealed water container on your sketching trip, you can paint your drawing immediately. This is a good way to practise showing realistic light and shade, and mixing lifelike colours.

Overlap colours to emphasize shadows or darker areas.

Dab wet paint with a tissue for a textured look.

Period styles

Every age has had a different general building style. These vary around the world. There are some examples below.

Ancient Egyptian (2600-30BC)

Classical Greek (600BC)

Islamic (700-1200)

Romanesque (1100-1200)

Gothic (1200-1400)

Byzantine (1600-1700)

Baroque (1700-1800)

Neo-Classical (1800-1900)

Neo-Gothic (late 1800s)

Modern (1900-)

Castles

Castles are huge, interesting buildings with long histories. They were built by powerful people such as kings and barons. They were used as a defence against raiding enemies as well as homes. This is why their walls are so thick and high.

Castles are not as hard to draw as they look. Find out below how to draw the castle shown on these two pages.

Distant mountains should be sketchy, small and not so heavily coloured as the castle.

Drawing the castle

Draw the basic block shapes of the castle walls, as shown here.

Now add the shapes of the towers, rubbing out any unwanted lines.

Add the roofs, turrets and windows, shown in blue.

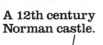

Add the drawbridge, staircase and roof flags. Sketch the stonework detail.

The detail on the side walls can be sketchy and pale.

The drawbridge is halfway down. Draw the angles carefully.

Different kinds of castles

There are lots of different styles of castles. The main picture shows a 14th century castle.

A 12th century Norman castle.

A 16th century Spanish castle.

A Gothic-style 19th century German castle. (A real-life fairytale castle.)

A 16th century English round-walled castle; its shape was to deflect cannonballs.

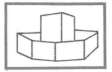
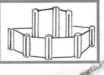
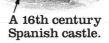
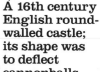
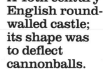

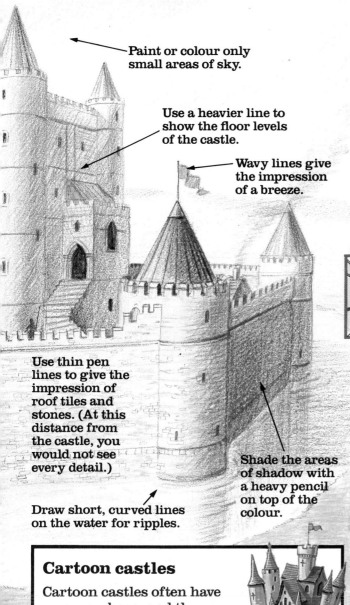

Paint or colour only small areas of sky.

Use a heavier line to show the floor levels of the castle.

Wavy lines give the impression of a breeze.

Use thin pen lines to give the impression of roof tiles and stones. (At this distance from the castle, you would not see every detail.)

Shade the areas of shadow with a heavy pencil on top of the colour.

Draw short, curved lines on the water for ripples.

Cartoon castles

Cartoon castles often have a narrow base, and the towers, turrets and flags are exaggerated. Sometimes they teeter on tall, narrow rocks. There is a fairytale castle to draw on page 104.

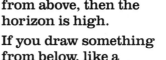

Perspective

Drawing things "in perspective" means drawing them the way your eyes see them. Perspective is based on the idea that things look smaller the further away they are. Pictures in perspective look real and three-dimensional (3-D), rather than flat.

When you look down a street with equal-sized buildings, the ones nearest look much bigger than those at the other end.

On a long street, the buildings seem to get closer together until they "meet". This imaginary meeting point is the "vanishing point".

There is often more than one vanishing point on the same picture. Lines that are parallel* to each other meet at the same vanishing point.

The vanishing points are on the horizon, an imaginary eye-level line.

If you draw something from above, then the horizon is high.

If you draw something from below, like a skyscraper, then the horizon is low.

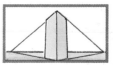

If you draw something looking straight at it, then the horizon can go through the middle.

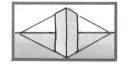

*Parallel lines are the same distance apart, like railway lines.

Fantasy buildings

Fantasy buildings are fun to invent and draw. The more detail you think of, the more convincing your fantasy world will be. Odd colours and strange figures and trees, for instance, can add life and atmosphere to your pictures. The ideas and techniques on these pages might help start you off.

Cartoons

Cartoons are not as easy as they look, because they are not strict copies of real things. Artists can use them to make jokes or comments (in newspaper cartoons, for instance) or to express imaginative ideas. Many of the buildings on these two pages are cartoons.

Professional cartoonists often draw quickly, using bold, incomplete lines. Try drawing a cartoon of your own house. Sketch the main shape loosely. Do not worry about getting lines too straight or filling in exact details.

Fairytale castle

In this drawing of a fairytale castle, lots of realistic details are either exaggerated or missed out altogether. There are lots of turrets, for instance, but no stonework or tiles on the roof.

The colours are unrealistic, with lots of pinks and purples. This helps to make the castle look magical.

Compare this drawing with the castle on the previous two pages. Try pin-pointing the things that make this one a fairytale castle.

Alien's house

This strange house belongs to an alien from a far-off planet. (There is more about imaginary space houses on page 117.)

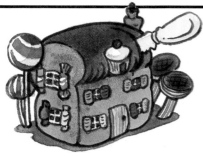

Fantasy ideas

This house is made out of different kinds of food. The main shape is easy to draw, but the details may take some time.

These cloud-people live in strange, fluffy cloud-houses. A huge umbrella over the top keeps the rain off.

This elves' workshop is full of machines and contraptions. You could use pale colours over a dark wash for the firelight.

Underwater city

This mysterious underwater city has been abandoned by its inhabitants. All sorts of sea creatures live here and the buildings are overgrown with seaweed.

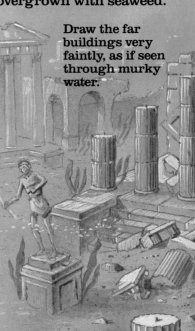

Draw the far buildings very faintly, as if seen through murky water.

Draw broken pillars, bits of statue lying on their sides and crumbling stairs.

Dark streaks for seaweed will give the impression of being underwater.

If you want your space house to look impressive, use a realistic style and paint or colour the picture very smoothly. Try to use muted or metallic colours.

For this picture, draw the nearest buildings first. Strong shadows and highlights and odd skies will help make your picture exciting and different.

Haunted house

An old, dark house can be made to look haunted and very creepy, and is great fun to draw. Ramshackle walls and roofs with slates missing make it look abandoned and mysterious. Oddly-shaped shadows, strange lights behind windows and big, dark trees all give your picture lots of spooky atmosphere.

Moonlight suggests witches and werewolves, and casts interesting light and shadow on the house (see opposite).

Graded amounts of white or black added to blue paint makes shades ranging from pale to deep blue. You can use these on different parts of the drawing.

Dramatic perspective

The perspective of this haunted house makes it look huge and terrifying. It is drawn as if you are looking from ground level, so the base looks wider than the top. (See page 103 for more about perspective.)

It is a bit more difficult to draw a house in this perspective, but it is worth trying, as your drawing will look very dramatic.

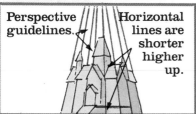

Perspective guidelines.

Horizontal lines are shorter higher up.

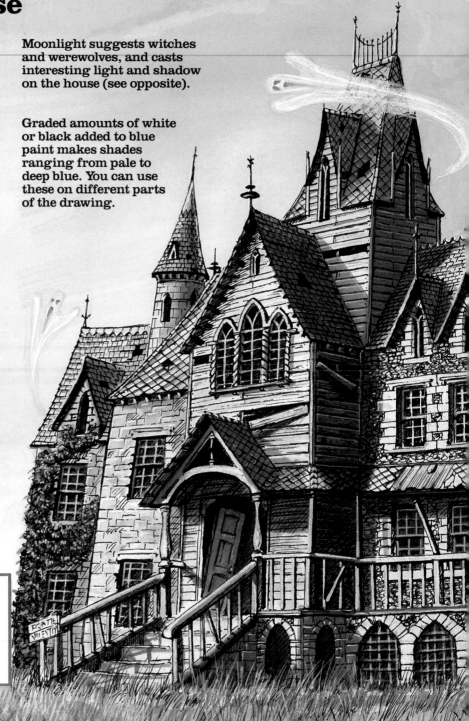

White streaks of paint for lightning will add atmosphere to your picture.

A strange light at a window will give the impression of a ghost. Fill half the window with shadow, in a vaguely human shape.

Look at the details on the roof and round the doors and windows. They all help to add a sinister feeling.

Large, dead trees beside the house look menacing. Make the branches thin and spiky, like fingers reaching out.

How to draw the house

First draw the basic shape of the house. Make sure that you have left enough space for windows and doors.

Add the turrets and the jutting sections of roof. Draw the lines straight at first. You can use them as guidelines to produce a more tumbledown look at a later stage.

Now draw the steps and the balcony at the front of the house.

Draw close lines across the roof for slates. When you colour the roof in, leave some black holes to show that some slates are missing.

Draw the wooden planks, leaving out a few. Draw the loose ones last, hanging down over the others.

Light and shadow

The light and shadow in your picture are important as they create atmosphere. Moonlight will make part of the house light, while the rest will be in deep shadow. This suggests that things are lurking there.

Drawing shadows

Shadows always fall away from the source of light, the sun or the moon. So all the shadows in one picture should go in the same direction.

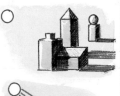

Something that is directly below the light has a short, squashed shadow.

Something standing at an angle to the light source will have a longer, more stretched shadow.

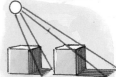

107

Ruins

Ruins can look ghostly and menacing, or sad and lonely. They make imaginative drawings but they can be quite difficult as they do not have a regular shape. The step-by-step instructions below show you how to make exciting, convincing drawings of ruins.

Buildings usually crumble at the top first, and particularly around any door and window openings.

← Draw the original shape of the window as a guide, then draw the ruined shape.

This way of shading, using ↙ lots of thin, criss-cross lines, is called cross-hatching.

A ruined church

This pencil drawing has a soft, atmospheric look. Varying the strength of line and shade can give the drawing texture and a feeling of depth.

Drawing the church

1. First, draw the original shape of the church faintly, to act as a guide. The lines can be rubbed out later.

2. Using a heavier line, draw the ruined shape of the church. (Rub out the first lines.)

3. Now draw the arches of the church and add details such as the windows and doors.

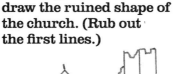

Adding atmosphere

Stormy skies and menacing trees add atmosphere to your drawing.

Old, crumbling graves make the church look even more abandoned.

Draw bits of fallen and broken stone and brick on the ground.

A bird perched on the window frame, or bushes growing in the doorway, make the church look deserted.

Draw the stones with a slightly wavering line, as if the edges have crumbled off. Add small black dots for moss.

A ruined street

After a disaster, such as an earthquake or a war, whole towns or cities can become almost complete ruins. The street below has suffered a great deal of damage and the houses have all been abandoned.

You could draw some furniture inside the houses. Use your own furniture as a guide.

Draw pictures and torn wallpaper on some walls, and roof rafters and rubble on the floors.

Draw large, black, scorched patches on the walls and round the windows.

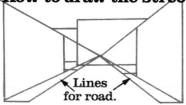

Use this picture of the street before damage as a guide for your own drawing.

You can sketch windows, doors and any interesting details on houses near you, and use them in your picture.

How to draw the street

Lines for road.

Draw two lines for the road. This will act as a guide when drawing the buildings in perspective (see page 103).

Draw the houses nearest to you first. Lightly sketch the original shapes as a guide before drawing the ruined shape.

Draw the internal walls and other details, working down the street. There will be heaps of debris lying about.

Ancient buildings

Temples or churches are often the most important and elaborate buildings in a civilization. You can find out on these pages how to draw four examples from around the world. The buildings date from around 1500BC to the Middle Ages.

Egyptian temple

Temples like this were ▶ built for many centuries when the Egyptians had a huge empire. The walls are covered with pictures of gods and goddesses.

1. Draw the main shape of the temple. Note that all walls slope inwards.

2. Now add the raised roof, the front towers, the gateway and the flagpoles.

3. Draw the columns and the wall pictures to complete the temple.

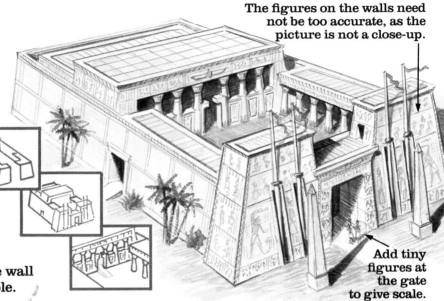

The figures on the walls need not be too accurate, as the picture is not a close-up.

Add tiny figures at the gate to give scale.

Incense was burned during sacred rituals, such as burials.

Mayan temple

◀ This 5th century pyramid-temple was built by the Maya people of Guatemala. Its ruins are still at the site of the Lost City of Rio Azul.

1. Draw the pyramid shape. Roughly plot then draw the cross-lines and steps.

2. Rub out the pyramid peak. Draw the top building in blocks.

3. Add the stairway and sketch in the wall paintings.

Gothic cathedral

Gothic cathedrals like this were built ▶ all over medieval Europe. The high, thin walls and turrets were richly carved.

1. **Draw the blocks which make up the main shape of the building.***

2. **Draw the roofs and turrets. Start at the front and work back.**

3. **Add the doors and windows. Then start to add the detail of the carved stonework.**

A lighter touch on the far side gives an impression of size and distance.

Greek temple

Temples like the one in this picture were built in Greece around the 5th century BC. The style has been copied in Europe right up to the present day. ▼

1. **Draw the main, rectangular shape. Be careful about the perspective.**

2. **Now draw the roof shape and mark in the tops and bottoms of columns.**

3. **Complete the columns and add the carved details on the front end of the building.**

If you draw upright lines in perspective (see page 103), a building may look as if it is leaning backwards. Architectural illustrators tend to draw upright lines almost vertical unless they want to create the effect of extreme height or scale. **111**

Skyscrapers and skylines

Skyscrapers are the tallest buildings in the world and they can make very dramatic pictures. They are quite easy shapes to draw but the perspective (see page 103) can be more difficult because they are so big.

A superhero's view

This is the way a city would look to a superhero swooping in to save people from disaster. Skyscrapers loom everywhere and the skyline in the distance is dominated by them.

All the pictures on these pages were airbrushed (see opposite).

1. Start by drawing straight lines as a perspective guide for the skyscrapers. They should be slightly closer together at the bottom.

2. Now draw the roofs and sides of the buildings. Keep opposite sides parallel. Try to picture how the street runs below.

3. Sketch in each floor of the skyscrapers. The lines appear to get closer together as you look down the buildings.

4. Work out where shadows will fall on the buildings and shade these areas. The shadows should be quite dark for an evening scene.

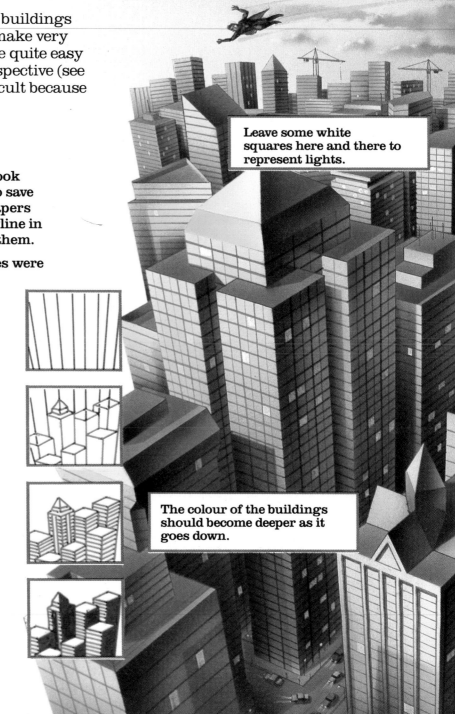

Leave some white squares here and there to represent lights.

The colour of the buildings should become deeper as it goes down.

*See page 21 for how to draw superheroes.

A different perspective

Drawing a skyscraper from below
– a worm's eye view (see page 103) –
makes it look very dramatic.

This time, you have to
draw the base very
wide. The sides
taper up to a
thin, dizzy
tip high
above.

1. Tiny
people
show the
building's
height. Draw
the floors
closer as
they go up.

2. White
streaks on
pale blue
walls
highlight
the building
and make it
look glassy.

3. Other
buildings
reflected
on the wall
heighten the
glassy look
and add
interest.

Drawing the skyline

Here the skyline shows the dark
outlines of the buildings. This is
called a silhouette.

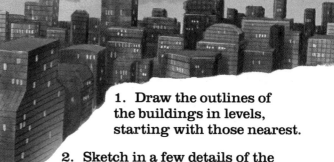

1. Draw the outlines of
the buildings in levels,
starting with those nearest.

2. Sketch in a few details of the
nearest buildings, to make
them less of a flat shape.

3. Colour everything in dark, muted
colours. Watery paint produces
the best effect.

Airbrushing

Many professional artists use an
airbrush to produce a smooth, even
finish to a picture.

The airbrush is connected
to a compressed air
supply which sprays a
mixture of air and paint
on to the drawing. Any
part the artist does not
want to colour is covered
with a clear plastic
called "masking film".

Airbrushing equipment is
expensive.* You can achieve
similar results if you apply
felt tips or paints smoothly.

*See page 126 for more about cheaper airbrushes

Airport

This page shows you how to plan and draw your own exciting, aerial-view picture of an airport. It is not as hard as it looks if you build up the picture in stages.

Composition

What artists decide to show in a drawing, and from which angle, is called the composition. For this airport scene, they might do several sketches from different angles to see which looks best. They could work from aerial photographs, or plans.

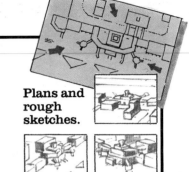

Plans and rough sketches.

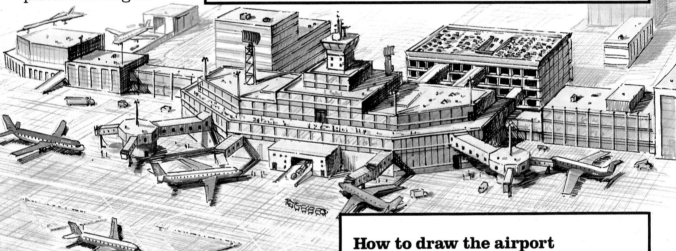

Emphasize flatness and distance by cross-hatching* runways and grass in perspective, as in this picture.

Draw long, bold, "whoosh" lines behind the plane taking off.

How to draw the airport

1. Sketch the basic shapes. You could make a perspective grid as a guide (see page 124).

2. Now draw the true shapes of the buildings. Add details such as the tower and windows.

3. Add the planes (see opposite) to bring the picture to life. Now add shadows and highlights.

*See page 108.

Railway station

This drawing of a 19th century railway station is quite hard to do, but if you work out the perspective accurately, your picture should be convincing. A pair of compasses will help you draw the roof arches.

You can leave the roof detail quite sketchy.

Smudge pen lines above the train with water for a smoky effect.

Small, sketchy figures give scale to the drawing.

There is a selection of trains you can draw below.

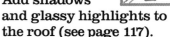

How to draw the station

First, draw perspective lines for the platform and the walls. They all go to a central vanishing point*.

Use compasses for the roof arches. Keeping the point in the same place, make each arc wider than the last.

Draw the trains, the wall detail and the benches. Add shadows and glassy highlights to the roof (see page 117).

Drawing trains and planes

These pictures might help you when drawing trains and planes. See page 119 for how to copy and enlarge the drawings using a grid.

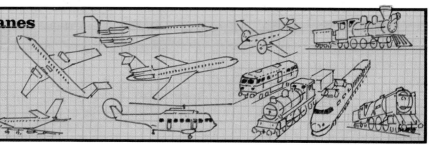

---

* See page 103.

Future cities

The future cities here are drawn in a comic book style, which uses bold, black line and large areas of flat colour. Dramatic shadows and highlights make this style atmospheric and lively. It is especially good for drawing futuristic scenes.

Space colony

This space colony is built under domes to protect people from an airless environment and from unbroken sunlight and heat.

Strong shadows along the dome's edge help to make it look 3-D.

Earth city of the future

In this future city, the huge population is housed in vast structures. Tiny trees and the traditional church show the scale of the new buildings. The picture below is divided into sections to show you how an artist might plan and draw this scene in comic book style.

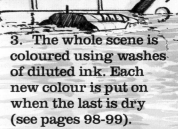

1. The artist plans the scene in pencil, checking composition* and perspective. A few door and window details are added.

2. Now everything is drawn over in waterproof ink. Finer details and shadows are added. Rough pencil lines are rubbed out.

3. The whole scene is coloured using washes of diluted ink. Each new colour is put on when the last is dry (see pages 98-99).

Bold white highlights on the domes makes them look as if they are under fierce light (see below).

The whole picture is tilted slightly to make it look dramatic and odd.

The light and shadow contrast strongly to make the scene look brightly lit.

The city details should be tiny, to give a sense of the size of the domes.

Even in the far future, some old buildings, such as this church, may be left intact.

4. The artist now highlights sunlit areas and adds shine to some buildings to make them look glassy. "Movement" lines are painted on the water and behind the small jet, above left.

Reflections and highlights

Artists use lots of different ways to highlight areas of their drawings. Some of them are shown below.

Unpainted white areas are planned at the drawing stage.

Streaks of white pencil can give a gentle, glassy sheen.

Lines of white paint produce a bold shine (see the domes above).

Black ink can show ripples and reflections in water and glass.

117

Space station

This is how a space station might look in the far distant future. Inside, there are huge living areas, vast hothouses and laboratories for space experiments. Solar panels provide power and there are busy docking areas for spaceships.

The space station houses many people. All the food is grown in the hothouses and trees provide oxygen to breathe. Strange plants collected from other planets are also grown.

Drawing the space station

The space station can be broken down into four main shapes: the central rod, an ellipse, a block and a pyramid for the nose.

← Ellipse shape

Draw the skeleton shape of the station first, starting with the rod and ellipse shape.

Build up the details, working from the back. As you complete each area, curve the edges of the station, rubbing out rough lines.

"Whoosh" lines give an idea of movement.

Paint thin streaks of white on the surfaces to give a glassy look.

E410

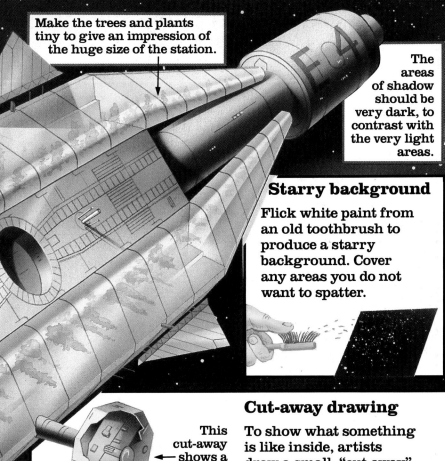

Make the trees and plants tiny to give an impression of the huge size of the station.

The areas of shadow should be very dark, to contrast with the very light areas.

Starry background

Flick white paint from an old toothbrush to produce a starry background. Cover any areas you do not want to spatter.

Enlarging drawings

Draw a grid of equal squares on tracing paper. Place the grid over the drawing.

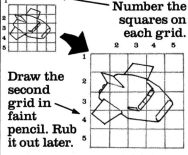

Number the squares on each grid.

Draw the second grid in faint pencil. Rub it out later.

Using a larger sheet of paper, draw a bigger grid with the same number of squares. Copy the drawing square-by-square on to it.*

Cut-away drawing

This cut-away shows a laboratory on the space station.

To show what something is like inside, artists draw a small, "cut-away" section on a drawing. It is a useful technique for showing how a machine works, or the inside of a building. The steps below show you how to use the cut-away technique.

How to draw cut-aways

Draw a rough plan of the inside of the section. (See pages 122-123 for more about plans.)

Draw the main shape of the section and sketch the inside, to get the right perspective.

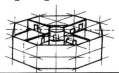

Draw the cut-away area. Rub out any inside details hidden by the walls and go over the part you can see in more detail.

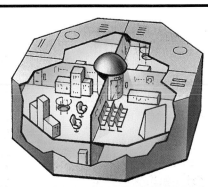

Special effects

Artists often use special techniques to make their drawings look funny or atmospheric. Some of them are shown on these two pages. You can use the colouring styles on any of your drawings.

Cartoons

You can use a bold cartoon technique to make fun drawings, such as the dancing skyscrapers shown here. The buildings have to be recognizable, although the angles are slightly distorted. The details can be sketchy.

Slightly curved edges make buildings look flexible. Add lots of bold movement lines.

You can add a face, or use windows as eyes and a door as a mouth to make buildings look like characters. Chimneys can be drawn as hats, and add ivy for hair.

Use a bold, clear line when drawing the basic shape.

Cartoon technique is often used to make a serious point. In this drawing, a chemical factory has been made into a monster, spouting pollution from its mouth.

Colouring styles

Some artists try to capture the overall atmosphere of a scene rather than emphasize the detail. This is called impressionism. The style is quite loose, although the drawing is still accurate. You can use the techniques shown below to create an impressionist quality.

This technique uses lots ▶ of watery paint. You would need to stretch art paper before beginning. Find out how to do this on page 127.

Pale, washy colours run together to create a misty effect.

Bold, obvious brush strokes give a painting a sense of urgency and excitement. You can also try this with felt tips or coloured pencils.

You could try pastels or coloured pencils for a similar effect.

There is often a great emphasis on the light and shadow of a scene.

You could try using lots of tiny dots of colour. Denser patches of dots can be used for shadows and details such as windows.

Floodlit building

This floodlit building was painted in white and shades of grey over a dark wash.

You could use a white pencil on black paper, instead. After shading, details are added in pen.

A pencil outline of the building will show up on a dark background and act as a guide.

Watery grey is used first, building up to strong, thick white for some details.

The railings are dark as the floodlights are beyond them. This gives the picture depth.

The shadows

As the building is lit from below, the shadows fall in the opposite direction to normal. Anything jutting out will cast a shadow upwards.

Light

Shadows fall upwards.

Drawing and using plans

All buildings start as a set of plans. After an architect has designed the building, plans are worked out and drawn accurately. On these pages you can see how to draw your own plans and use them to make a model.

Technical drawing

The neat, detailed drawing style used for plans is called technical drawing.

Building plans are flat drawings of a 3-D shape. Some of the tools used for technical drawing are shown below.

Compasses, set squares and rulers for drawing arcs, angles and straight lines.

A flexi-curve can be adjusted to draw any kind of curve.

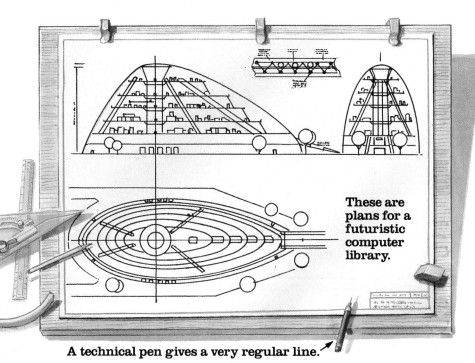

These are plans for a futuristic computer library.

A technical pen gives a very regular line.

Drawing plans

There are three main plan-drawing steps.

1. All measurements are worked out and a scale (see below) is set.

2. Information is gathered about all features such as windows, doors, wall thicknesses and even stoves and sinks. Rough plans are then drawn.

3. The finished plan is drawn to scale, using standard symbols for some features. Several elevations (see below) are usually shown.

Scale

A suitable scale is worked out for a plan, depending on the building's size. A scale of 1:100 means that 1cm on the plan represents 1m (or 1:12 is an inch to a foot).

Elevations

Most plans show a building from two or more viewpoints. If the front and the side are shown, for example, these are called the front and side elevations.

Drawing your home

Follow the steps here to make a plan of the inside of your home.

1. First note the length and width of the rooms and corridors of your home. Use a tape measure rather than a ruler.

2. Do a rough sketch to help you position everything. Then work out a simple scale to be used on the finished drawing.

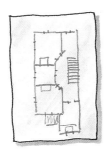

3. Measure windows and doors, noting their positions and direction of opening. Note the number of stairs.

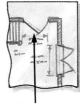

Door opens inwards.

4. Do the final drawing. Add features such as the stove.

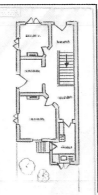

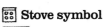 Stove symbol

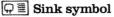 Sink symbol

Making a model

You could invent your own building and make a model of it. You may find it helpful to draw a scale plan and elevations for it first.

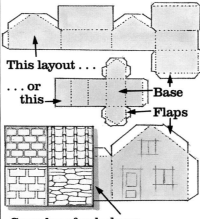

This layout . . .

. . . or this

Base

Flaps

Samples of rub-down (transfer) details.

Make sure all shadows go in the same direction.

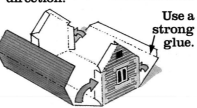

Use a strong glue.

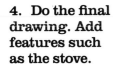

Once you feel confident about drawing plans and making models, you can tackle quite complicated shapes.

Make your drawing of the model on thin cardboard so that it stands up firmly. You will need scissors and glue.

1. Lay out the building in a straight line, or around a base, whichever you prefer. Draw flaps down each open side for glueing together later.

2. Now draw details such as doors, windows and roof tiles. You can buy rub-down (transfer) bricks, stones and tiles if you prefer.

3. Paint or colour your drawing, adding shadows and highlights. You can use paint wash to build up a textured look on walls and roofs.

4. Cut the building out. Fold the flaps and glue the building together. Paint a base on a piece of cardboard and glue your building on to that.

Reconstructions and impressions

Artists are often asked to draw reconstructions of ancient or ruined buildings. The drawings can be used by historians or archaeologists, or as museum displays to show how the buildings looked when they were whole.

Sometimes artists' impressions are done of a building which does not yet exist. The drawings are used for various purposes, such as advertising.

Reconstructing ruins

This is a reconstruction of a Viking settlement. Before drawing anything, the artist studies any plans and photographs, and may visit the site too.

The first sketches are drawn in perspective, using a perspective plan (see bottom of page). You could draw the scene, using the sketch below.

Viking trading ship.

Details of everyday life, such as clothing, transport and building materials are carefully researched. These bring the scene to life.

Making a perspective plan

The artist draws a grid over the original plan and plots each building.* A second grid with an equal number of squares is then drawn in perspective.

Number the squares.

Make this grid bigger if needed.

The positions of the buildings are transferred to the second grid on the corresponding squares.

The artist now has a perspective plan. You can try this yourself.

New buildings

This artist's impression of a modern "designer" house has been drawn using architects' plans and a bit of imagination. You can try drawing it yourself.

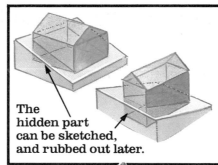

Buildings on slopes

Buildings are always level. On a hill, part of the base of a building is hidden under the ground. Imagine its complete form before drawing a building such as this.

The hidden part can be sketched, and rubbed out later.

Draw the basic block shapes in perspective. The eye level is below the horizon*.

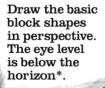

Sketch the hidden corner of the base.

Dark trees and shadows emphasize corners and add depth.

With impressions, you can choose the angle that the sunlight strikes the building.

Interiors

The insides of buildings can be hard to draw. The scene is close-up, and only part of the whole structure is visible. This means that there are no basic block shapes to build up and the angles are difficult to draw in perspective. This picture shows part of the inside of the house above.

Draw the skeleton shape of the room first. Add the pillars and stairs.

Deep shadows down the edges of the pillars will help them look 3-D.

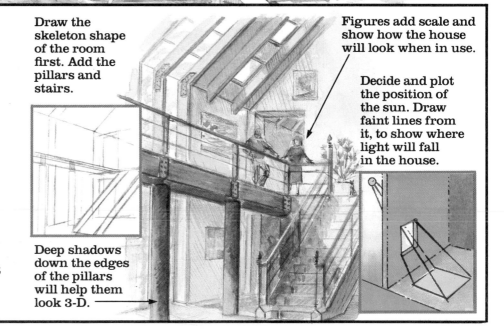

Figures add scale and show how the house will look when in use.

Decide and plot the position of the sun. Draw faint lines from it, to show where light will fall in the house.

*See page 103.

Tips and materials

When learning to draw, you need not spend a lot of money on equipment. Choosing the right drawing tools and paper, and learning some basic techniques will help you make a good start.

Choosing drawing tools

The kind of drawing tool you use depends on the style you want. A pen or pencil, for instance, is best for detailed line drawing. A mixture of some of the items below is ideal.

◄ **Pencils** range from very hard to very soft (9H to 7B*). It is best to buy a hard (2H) and a medium (HB) pencil for lines, and a soft (3B) pencil for shading.

Felt or fibre tip pens can be used for ▶ line drawing and colouring. Fibre tips give a thinner line while felt tips are good for large areas of colour.

◄ **Coloured pencils** can give lines of varying thickness and colour strength. They also show up well on coloured paper. Some can double as paints.

Wax crayons, pastels, chalks and ▶ charcoal can be blended for a softer look. They are good for large-scale drawings.

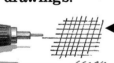

◄ **Pens** are widely available, ranging from ballpoints to fine technical drawing pens. They are good for all line drawing.

Watercolour paints can be mixed to ▶ produce a wide range of colours. Buy two paintbrushes – a medium one for general use and a thin one for detail.

Paper

There is a large range of paper available. Most stationery shops sell basic sketch pads, and these are fine for most purposes. The best quality watercolour paper is usually only available from art shops. Do not paint on very thin paper.

Loose-leaf, plain paper is fine for most drawings.➡

Rougher sketch paper is better for paint.➡

Rough water-colour paper is ideal for paint, but expensive.➡

Airbrushes

If you want to experiment with airbrush technique, a slightly cheaper version, called a modeller's airbrush, is available in art or model shops. They use cans of compressed air instead of costly compressors.

*H stands for hard and B stands for black.

Stretching paper

If you use a lot of paint, it is best to buy sketch or watercolour paper. Stretch paper before beginning, or it will wrinkle when the paint dries.

To stretch paper, you need a board, brown gummed parcel strip, a sponge and water.

1. Measure and tear off the gummed strips – one length for each side of the paper.

2. Wet (but do not soak) the paper thoroughly under a cold tap with a sponge.

> There should be no pools of water on the paper.

3. Place the paper flat on the board. Working clockwise, tape the edges quickly with dampened gummed strip.

4. Wipe off excess water with a damp sponge. Leave to dry naturally. Do not use while wet.

> Any wrinkles should smooth out when dry.

5. Leave the paper on the board while you paint. Cut it out carefully with a sharp knife when dry.

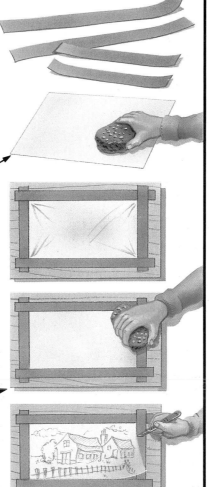

Fixative sprays

Fixative puts a hard, clear finish on a drawing so that it does not fade or smudge. It also allows you to work over a drawing's surface without spoiling existing patterns.

Mouth diffuser

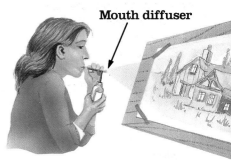

Fixative is available in art shops. You can blow it through a mouth diffuser, or buy a spray can. Avoid breathing the fumes.

Other equipment

Rulers with built-in stencils of shapes or lines can be very useful for your drawings.

Cotton buds can smudge and blend crayons, pastels and chalks.

Plastic erasers rub out pencil lines cleanly. Putty erasers can be twisted to reach tiny areas.

127

Index

Chris Chapman is represented by Maggie Mundy Agency.

First published in 1992 by Usborne Publishing Ltd, Usborne House, 83-85 Saffron Hill, LONDON EC1N 8RT

Copyright © Usborne Publishing Ltd 1992

The name Usborne and the device 🎈 are Trade Marks of Usborne Publishing Ltd.

Printed in Belgium.

First published in America March 1993